"You don't mind…instructing me?"

Daniel's voice dropped, low and husky and aroused, and Lace wondered at his reaction. Was he really so nervous at the prospect of making love to her? Her heart softened.

No! Not her heart. She would not get emotionally involved with Daniel Sawyers. Their worlds were too different for them to ever harmonize. She would not get drawn in by him, by his need. He was just a man, as flawed as any man.

"Daniel, do you think you can accept a brief affair with me?"

Dear Reader,

Happy Valentine's Day! And what better way to celebrate Cupid's reign than by reading six brand-new Desire novels...?

Putting us in the mood for sensuous love is this February's MAN OF THE MONTH, with wonderful Dixie Browning offering us the final title in her THE LAWLESS HEIRS miniseries in *A Knight in Rusty Armor.* This alpha-male hero knows just what to do when faced with a sultry damsel in distress!

Continue to follow the popular Fortune family's romances in the Desire series FORTUNE'S CHILDREN: THE BRIDES. The newest installment, *Society Bride* by Elizabeth Bevarly, features a spirited debutante who runs away from a business-deal marriage...into the arms of the rugged rancher of her dreams.

Ever-talented Anne Marie Winston delivers the second story in her BUTLER COUNTY BRIDES, with a single mom opening her home and heart to a seductive acquaintance, in *Dedicated to Deirdre.* Then a modern-day cowboy renounces his footloose ways for love in *The Outlaw Jesse James,* the final title in Cindy Gerard's OUTLAW HEARTS miniseries; while a child's heartwarming wish for a father is granted in Raye Morgan's *Secret Dad.* And with *Little Miss Innocent?* Lori Foster proves that opposites *do* attract.

This Valentine's Day, Silhouette Desire's little red books sizzle with compelling romance and make the perfect gift for the contemporary woman—you! So treat yourself to all six!

Enjoy!

Joan Marlow Golan
Senior Editor, Silhouette Desire

Please address questions and book requests to:
Silhouette Reader Service
U.S.: 3010 Walden Ave., P.O. Box 1325, Buffalo, NY 14269
Canadian: P.O. Box 609, Fort Erie, Ont. L2A 5X3

LITTLE MISS INNOCENT?
LORI FOSTER

SILHOUETTE *Desire*®
Published by Silhouette Books
America's Publisher of Contemporary Romance

SILHOUETTE BOOKS

ISBN 0-373-76200-3

LITTLE MISS INNOCENT?

Copyright © 1999 by Lori Foster

This edition published by arrangement with Harlequin Books S.A.

® and TM are trademarks of Harlequin Books S.A., used under license.
Trademarks indicated with ® are registered in the United States Patent
and Trademark Office, the Canadian Trade Marks Office and in other
countries.

Printed in U.S.A.

LORI FOSTER

lives in a small town in Ohio with her high school sweet-heart (whom she was smart enough to marry twenty years ago) and their three sons—all very special, incredibly wonderful guys (not that she's biased). The only thing she loves more than writing and reading romance is being with her family. You can write to Lori at P.O. Box 854, Ross, OH 45061.

To Bonnie Tucker
Your caring, your openness and your incredible humor
are so very much appreciated. It's easy to see why
you're a friend to so many, and why I'm so glad
you're a friend to *me*.

One

No. It couldn't be. Daniel rubbed his eyes and tried to deny the highly sensual sight that faced him. But when he looked again, Lace McGee still filled his vision.

It had been a long endless shift, in an even longer endless day. Now it was nearly nine o'clock. Time for him to go home. Though the emergency room still roared with chaos, his brain felt numb, his body dulled with fatigue. He wanted to walk out the sliding-glass doors and to his car, but there *she* stood, blocking the way by her mere presence. Just the sight of her seemed taunting and tempting. She was a thorn in his side, a pain in the butt… Hell, there didn't seem to be a single part of his anatomy that Lace didn't bother in one way or another.

He would simply ignore her, he decided. He stepped away from the front desk and waved goodbye to a group of nurses who hustled past, sending him spoony sidelong glances. They were ever persistent, but gently so, with discretion, respecting his wishes as a bachelor to remain a bachelor. Not like Lace, who forced her way into his thoughts whether he wanted her there or not. She didn't like it when he tried to ignore her—as if any man actually could. She was too damned intrinsically female, too...*noticeable*.

He didn't mean to, but he glanced at her again, and then he couldn't look away. His palms began to sweat. His glasses fogged.

The cold evening wind sent her dark cloak swirling as white snow blew in behind her, making her entrance seem dramatically staged. Was she here to harass him again, to tease him until his body warred with his brain and his resolve crumbled? His heartbeat quickened as it always did, even as his customary scowl fell into place. He would not let her win.

Then she stepped farther inside and the doors whispered shut behind her.

Without the winter night as a backdrop, he realized Lace wasn't standing as tall as usual. Her face seemed pale rather than radiant, her white-blonde hair looked bedraggled, and as he looked lower, he saw a large tear in her black slacks and blood covering her leg. His heart gave a painful lurch at the sight of that slim pale leg, and he jerked out of his stupor. A nurse had already reached her by the time Daniel roared up to her side.

"What the hell happened?"

The nurse looked startled, but Lace only gave him her patented killer grin, though it didn't measure up to her usual knock-him-on-his-can standard. "Hello there, Danny." Her gaze skimmed his face, then his body, and her voice lowered to a husky whisper. "My, you're looking in fine form today."

She deliberately threw him with ridiculous compliments, and he always allowed himself to be thrown, damn her. But not this time. Not with her so obviously hurt. He took her arm to steady her, then reached to lift her cloak and look behind her where most of the damage seemed to be. She slapped at his hands, but his determination overrode her efforts.

He dropped the cape and in a softer, more controlled tone asked, "What happened, Lace?"

She leaned into him—which he expected since that was another of her ploys to drive him insane. This time he didn't step away from her, but held her a little closer. Her body felt warm and soft against his. When she looked up at him, her expression was serious rather than flirtatious. He didn't like it; this wasn't the Lace he was used to.

Lace didn't seem to notice. "I got bit. By a big stupid neighbor's dog."

She looked shaken and he said easily, offering her more support, "The neighbor is big and stupid, or the dog is?"

"Both."

Without missing a beat, he turned to the nurse. "Notify the police and health authorities, then join us." She nodded and hurried away. Daniel's gaze came back to Lace. Damn, but he didn't want to feel concern for her. He didn't want to feel anything. He didn't even like the woman.

He merely *lusted* her.

Her pants were a mess, shredded from just above the back upper thigh, to the front of her right knee. Another nurse had hurried forward with a wheelchair, but Daniel waved her away. "I don't think she can sit." Then to

Lace, "Should we get a stretcher, or can you make it to a room?"

Her beautiful eyes narrowed. "I can make it."

He recognized that stubborn set to her jaw. It was the same stubborn look she wore whenever she wanted him to see things her way, which was usually whenever she got around him. And because she was his sister's best friend and they were a close family, that seemed to be more often than not lately. Which explained why he was slowly—and painfully—going crazy.

With his arm around her narrow waist, and his other hand supporting her elbow, he took her to the first empty examining room he found. "Where, exactly, did you get bit?" He had to control his tone with an effort. The idea of an animal attacking her made his gut clench and his heart pound. He didn't like her, didn't approve of her, but she was a delicate woman, more feminine than any he'd ever known. The thought of her soft flesh being torn by sharp teeth was obscene.

Amazingly, her cheeks colored and she looked away. "In the butt."

Daniel knew embarrassment when he saw it, but he'd never have expected it of Lace. Good grief, the woman was a sex therapist, renowned for her books on sexual enlightenment and her late-night radio talk show. A self-professed expert on male/female relationships, she talked openly and without hesitation about every private subject known to man. Of course, as a doctor, he'd known plenty of other therapists. But Lace was different. She was certainly no Dr. Joyce Brothers.

So surely being bitten in a less than auspicious place couldn't be what bothered her. Daniel didn't even try to understand her. He'd done that numerous times, and it only raised his blood pressure and gave him a headache.

Exasperated with himself, he took off his glasses to polish them on a sleeve, giving himself a moment to think. "Tell me what happened."

"I had just come in from a late appointment—"

"An appointment, huh?" He shoved his glasses back onto the bridge of his nose.

"Get your brain out of the gutter, Doctor. Or was it your libido that went slumming there?"

He scowled. She always had some smart remark that thoroughly outdid his own, and she never explained herself. Not that he really expected her to, but still...

"I put my purse away then went down to the lobby to check the mail. And somehow a cat had gotten into the building. It ran behind me, the neighbor's dog tried to go through me and, like an idiot, I turned to see if the cat was all right, giving the mutt a prime target. But he'd never acted aggressive before, so I didn't really consider that he'd bite me."

"Damn. Hold still."

"No." She twisted around to stare at him, and panic edged her tone. "What are you doing?"

"Cutting these pants off you so we can see the damage."

"We?" There was so much nervous sarcasm in her voice, he almost hesitated. "Are you using the royal vernacular now? Because you're the only one looking. I sure as certain can't see a thing."

"Hush, Lace. The nurse will be right back."

"I don't want to hush!" Her voice rose to a squeak as he peeled the bloody pants away. "I demand a different doctor!"

"Well, you've got me." Daniel winced at the damage done to her beautiful skin. Whatever color her panties had once been, they were now stained dark by Lace's blood. The dog's teeth had punctured several places, and then actually torn through her skin, probably when she pulled away. He carefully swabbed at the blood, making certain to wipe away from the wound. His hand shook and he hated himself for it. He'd seen plenty of female bottoms, but none had been hers. Of course, all those nights when he'd dreamed of being this close to her bare, perfectly rounded backside, Lace had been beside herself with desire—only for him. She most certainly hadn't been in pain.

He swabbed at a particularly vicious tear and Lace howled.

Daniel spared her a glance, but his attention remained on caring for her. Past grievances seemed to drift away. Seeing her hurt made him hurt, as well. But she was his sister's best friend, so he reasoned that was acceptable.

"Shh. I know it stings. And you're definitely going to need stitches. The wound is too large to leave open, especially over a stress point like this."

"Damn you, Daniel, stop looking at me!"

"I have to look at you to assess the damage. Whatever modesty you're trying to protect is still intact, I assure you."

"I want a plastic surgeon!"

That gave him pause. "Lace, the scarring will be minimal, and being where it's located, it won't even be seen by the...casual...observer."

He ran out of words and his insides twisted. "Surely it's not that big a deal. Even the briefest bathing suit will cover it. But then, that's not the issue here, is it?" He watched her face, keeping his own expression carefully impassive. "It would be awkward, but I imagine if two lovers were very creative, the scar might be seen. How often do you intend to be displaying this part of your anatomy for male appreciation, Lace?''

She'd gasped with his first words and now her color rose. ''That's certainly none of your business, you damned lecher!''

The nurse walked in and came to a dead stop at Lace's accusing tone. To Daniel's relief, Lace snapped her teeth together and held back any further barrage of outrage. She turned her face away, crossing her arms over her head, and Daniel imagined her stubborn little nose pressed hard against the stiff, cloth-covered table.

He tried for patience—which always seemed in short supply whenever Lace McGee came around. She had a knack for bringing out the worst in him, and he hated himself for allowing her that advantage. He'd learned control long ago; he'd become a master at hiding his feelings and taking care of business because it had been vital to do so. After his mother had died and his father had fallen apart, someone had needed to see to his younger brother and sister. Daniel had elected himself.

But years of self-training and rigid discipline seemed to melt away whenever this particular woman showed up. He took a deep breath and nodded to the nurse.

''Finish getting her pants off so we can make sure there's no other bites. I'll be back in just a minute.''

Lace made a choking sound at his order, but kept her thoughts, and her words, to herself. Just as well, he decided, because objections in this case wouldn't have done her any good. He was a doctor, now her doctor, whether she liked it or not.

He stepped out of the room and collapsed against the wall beside the door. The fatigue had left him. He felt wide-awake, charged, full of determination and renewed purpose, and the reason didn't sit well with him at all.

She was a liberal—a sinfully enticing, sexy liberal and a horrible influence on his sister Annie. After twenty-five years of being a sweet-natured tomboy, Annie was suddenly stubborn and willful and more often than not when he saw her, she looked too…female, too…

His brain shied away from the word *sexy* when applied to the sister he'd practically raised on his own.

But he knew it was true. Annie now attracted men in droves, and he didn't like it. But Annie did. Just recently, Annie had gotten pulled into a melee when a brawl had erupted at a local singles' bar. She'd been picked up by the police. Before that, she'd never even been in a bar. He still didn't know what the hell she'd been doing there.

But he did know that it was somehow Lace's fault. She'd turned his sister in a willful femme fatale and she'd affected his libido to such a degree he didn't recognize himself anymore. Hell, she could probably adversely affect the morals of the whole human race with her candid, brassy way. She talked openly of sex, flirted with him outrageously simply to provoke him, and dressed for effect. She enjoyed making him squirm. They were opposites in every way, and she loved driving that fact home whenever it would make him most uncomfortable.

But what she didn't realize was that he'd become addicted to her unique form of torture. After all, he was a man, and he couldn't help reacting to her as such. When she wasn't around, he thought of her, dreamed of her. Yes, he disapproved of the life-style she led. As a rational, intelligent, responsible man, he abhorred sexual promiscuity—yet she epitomized that standard with her every breath. When he allowed common sense to guide him, he disliked her immensely.

But that didn't keep him from wanting her. Of all the women in all the world, he wanted Lace McGee so badly he could no longer sleep at night. He burned with wanting her, and resistance became more difficult every day.

And now, for the first time in his life, he hadn't been able to remain totally detached when treating a patient. With the very fiber of his being, he'd been aware of touching Lace, seeing Lace, worrying for Lace. That fact struck at the bone of his professional pride. He should get away from her now, while he still had his integrity.

But he'd be damned if he'd let anyone else in there with her.

Lace wished she could hide somewhere, anywhere. Under a mossy rock would do just fine. Of all the doctors to be on call tonight, why did Daniel have to be the one to see her first? And why, when he so obviously disdained everything about her, did he insist on taking care of her? If he knew the depths of mortification she suffered by the circumstances, he'd be more than a little amused. The damn Neanderthal. The damn *gorgeous,* uptight, prudish Neanderthal.

Lace tightened her fingers in her hair and winced when the nurse tugged her slim-fitting slacks over her backside. "So, you and Doctor Sawyers know each other?"

That almost brought a grin. Here she was in the most ignominious position of her entire twenty-seven years, and the nurse displayed signs of jealousy. Lace knew the gossip would be all over the hospital in short order, but at the moment, she didn't care. She lifted her head to face the nurse and noted that she was a pretty woman, young and dark-eyed. Lace narrowed her gaze. "Dan is my best friend's brother.'' *And a totally obnoxious fellow.*

''Doctor Sawyers prefers to be called Daniel.''

Lace dropped her head back onto the table. ''Yeah, well, I prefer to annoy him. So I call him a variety of things.''

''Then you two aren't…involved?''

Ha. Fat chance of that when Daniel thought of her as a loose woman with no morals. She could still remember the first time she'd met him—not because she was still hurt over it, she assured herself. Only because narrow-minded judgment angered her.

Daniel hadn't shown the kindness or politeness or intelligence Annie had bragged of. No, the big oaf had turned up his nose at her and drawn an immediate and erroneous conclusion based on her career and appearance.

She was used to men doing that, though most of them assumed she was easy and tried to put the make on her. She'd learned over the years how to quickly correct those assumptions.

But Daniel had decreed her unfit and not only hadn't he wanted her in his bed, he hadn't wanted her anywhere around Annie. Lucky for her, Annie had a mind of her own, and she gleefully disobeyed big brother's orders.

Which gave Daniel another sin to lay at her door— the corruption of his twenty-five-year-old *baby* sister.

Of course, Lace hadn't helped to dissuade Daniel from his ridiculous notions. At first, she'd allowed him his beliefs because it rankled her that he thought so little of her simply because of her profession and her flamboyant looks. As if she could help the way she looked, she thought with a self-directed snort. She had her mother's vivid coloring and curvy figure, which had caused her endless grief but no shame.

Her work, on the other hand, was important, and as much a source of pride for her as his own profession. She helped people with their traumas. She made a difference, the same as he did. *Not that he'd ever see it that way.*

The nurse cleared her throat in impatience, and Lace replied, ''No, we're not involved.''

''I'm glad.'' The woman's voice was suddenly lighter, friendlier. ''Just about every single woman in this hospital has tried to get his attention. But he's always so serious. Not that any of us has given up hope.''

Actually, Daniel went beyond serious. Lace would have described him as funereal. Teasing him had become a form of retribution, turning his crank and pushing the buttons that got him steamed. Especially when he tried to be so somber and sophisticated about his anger. But lately, it had turned into a contest. Just once, she wanted to elicit an emotion from Daniel other than cold disdain and sarcasm. She wanted him to yell passionately, to react with fire. But that would never happen. The good doctor had a patent on sobriety.

''You know...'' Lace twisted so she could see the woman better, and an evil thought took root in her brain. It was terribly mean, but he deserved it, the self-righteous prig.

''Dan doesn't particularly like shy women. And he pretends to be a stick in the mud, but I know better. He likes an aggressive woman who isn't afraid to say what she wants, to tell him how she feels and how she wants to make him feel. Maybe all of you have just been too subtle.''

''Do you really think so?''

Lace grinned at her hopeful tone. "Trust me. Give him your best shot. He'll love all the attention."

Daniel walked back in then and, without a word to Lace, began preparing a shot. She could feel the cool air on her backside and gave a sigh of grateful relief when the nurse, now watching Daniel with a calculating eye, pulled a sheet over her. She stared at the back of Daniel's dark head. "What are you doing?"

"I'm going to give you an injection of lidocaine to numb your…the area, and then I'll stitch you up."

"Daniel…"

"Do you have the name of the dog's owner? The police will want to know and we need to fill out a dog-bite card."

"Forget it. I know the guy and I know the dog, and he's not really a bad dog, he just got overly excited."

"Lace." He turned to face her and his expression was grave. "What if the dog got excited around a kid? What happened to you could have been ten times worse with a small child."

"You're right. I'm sorry."

Daniel looked surprised at her quick agreement. His dark brows raised a fraction, and then he nodded.

Lace pondered the problem. Something had to be done. Just the thought of that dog sinking his teeth into a child chilled her to the bone. But though the dog was a pain, always barking and obviously too undisciplined, she also knew the man was lonely, the dog his only friend. "What will happen?"

"I'm not sure. First we'll make certain the dog has had all his shots."

"He has. The owner hurried to assure me of that after he got the dog to turn me loose."

Daniel winced. "Damn." His expression was unreadable, but Lace thought she saw a bit of sympathy. Impossible.

"I can't believe you're not mad about this." As Daniel spoke, he moved behind her and lifted the sheet. Lace wanted to die. She wanted to tell him to close his eyes, to wear blinders; she did not want to be vulnerable with this man. She began chattering to distract herself.

"I'm not happy to have gotten bitten, but it was an accident. The dog isn't normally vicious, in fact, it's still more a puppy than not. It's just so darn big. Maybe it should go to an obedience school or something. He's usually such a nice big ugly dog. And— Ouch!"

"I'm sorry."

He didn't sound sorry and she gave him a suspicious frown. "That hurt."

"You'll be numb in a minute." His gaze, damn him, remained glued to her backside. "So, how did you get here, by the way?"

Though she knew he asked only to distract her, she appreciated his efforts. It wasn't like Daniel to treat her with consideration, but then she supposed this was his doctor mode and he took his work very seriously. "This nice guy who was close by gave me a ride. I couldn't drive myself, and he had a big back seat, and vinyl upholstery in his car, so I figured I couldn't do much damage…"

"You rode in here with a stranger?"

The nurse was all ears, so Lace couldn't say precisely what she wished. She wanted to slap him, hard, for his damned presumptions and biased opinions of her. She did the next best thing. She grinned at him.

"Yeah. He was a real sweetheart. He offered to stay and wait for me, but I told him not to bother. He took my number so he could check on me later."

Daniel stared at her, his expression a cross between outrage, disbelief and sheer disgust. His lips were flattened together and his dark brows lowered behind his glasses. His disappointment was plain, but resigned, as if he expected no better of her. Lace tried to laugh, but couldn't quite pull it off. Damn him for always judging her. The man who'd given her the lift had to be around seventy and he'd had his wife of a similar age with him. She'd seen them both in the apartment complex many times, and on the trip to the hospital, they'd doted on her as if she'd been their only grandchild.

His censure hurt, and she heard herself saying, "It's not really like you think—"

But he cut her off. "It doesn't matter, Lace. How you live your life is of no concern to me."

She should have known better than to try to explain to him, the discriminating prude. He didn't want to know the truth about her. And until this moment, she hadn't cared. She decided it was the loss of blood that had temporarily rendered her sensitive to his censure. He was only a man, like many other unenlightened men, and his opinion didn't amount to a hill of beans.

In a sweet tone she said, "Did you expect me to limp in, Daniel, trailing blood in my wake?"

He ignored her. "When was the last time you had a tetanus shot?"

His lack of reaction deflated her. "I have no idea."

He took care of that in short order, only this time she didn't even flinch. Daniel still scowled, but there was also a look of concern on his face and Lace wondered at the seldom seen view. She knew what an excellent doctor he was. Not only did Annie brag on him constantly, but Lace visited the hospital often with her—especially if she knew Annie would be seeing Daniel—

and Lace had witnessed the amount of respect given him, the way patients responded to him. He was a wonderful doctor, a sinfully handsome man, and he disapproved of her mightily.

At present, he was busy studying her bottom in great detail. Her eyes nearly crossed at the discomfort of it.

"You're a real mess, Lace. We'll need about fifty subcuticular stitches—"

"Excuse me?" That sounded rather horrific and it unnerved her enough to counteract her embarrassment. She twisted her head around to watch him.

"Stitches in the underneath layer," Daniel explained, his fingers lightly exploring though she couldn't feel a thing, could only watch as his large hand coasted over her exposed flesh. "Another fifty on top. You won't be able to sit for a while, and you should try to keep any stress off the area."

"No deep knee bends, huh?"

Nervousness made her something of a smart-ass, but she couldn't seem to help herself. Daniel didn't appear to mind this time. "I'll give you a prescription for pain and one for oral antibiotics. I'll need to see you again in forty-eight hours to change the dressing, then after that, if all looks well, you can change the dressing yourself. The nurse will write out instructions for you to use a mixture of half-strength hydrogen peroxide. You'll want to watch for signs of infection, increasing pain, redness, swelling. There's going to be a lot of bruising."

"There goes my photo shoot."

Daniel made a sound of disgust, and Lace hid her smile. He'd started to sound too detached there for a moment, but she'd easily brought him back around.

They sat in silence for few moments, other than Daniel and the nurse murmuring to each other as he put in the stitches. Lace tried to think of other things. Unfortunately, every other thing she thought of still involved her with her pants off and Daniel looking at her.

"So if your savior left already, how do you plan to get home?"

The suddenness of his voice, the growling tone, made her jump. "I hadn't thought about it. I was more concerned with getting here at the time. But I don't look forward to throwing myself facedown in the back of a taxi, if that's what you want to know! Especially given the fact you ruined my slacks."

"If you recall, it was the dog that took a hunk out of you and your pants, not me. But I can give you some scrubs to wear home. That's not a problem."

He stared at Lace a moment more while she struggled to turn on her side and keep the sheet in place at the same time. He looked annoyed and angry and then he threw up his arms. "I suppose I'll just have to drive you home."

Lace stared, not at all amused. "You're kidding, right?"

"My shift actually ended just as you came in. I'm ready to leave, so it won't be any bother. And as you've pointed out to me many times, I drive a disgustingly sedate sedan with a *big back seat*." His gaze scanned her from head to toe. "You'll fit."

Lace didn't know what to think. On the one hand, Daniel was a very conscientious fellow. It could just be that he felt somehow obligated, regardless of his personal dislike of her, to see her settled safely. After all, he'd made her his patient, and she and Annie were very good friends, despite his edict to the contrary. He loved his little sister like crazy, so he wouldn't want her upset. But somehow it felt like more than that. And under no condition did she want to be alone with Daniel when she wasn't up to snuff. He'd make verbal mincemeat out of her, and she couldn't accept the defeat. Right now she ached all over, and she still suffered lingering humiliation. She wasn't in proper form to do battle with the big bad doctor.

"I could call Annie instead."

"Annie and Max have gone Christmas shopping. The malls are having a midnight sale, and Annie will make Max use every minute till then."

"Oh." Max was the middle brother. A real Lothario, but also a sweetheart, when someone understood him. "I forgot."

"Then you already knew?"

She nodded absently. "Max had invited me along." Then she slanted Daniel a look, realizing what he would say and wanting to beat him to the punch. Usually, that was her only defense against his criticism. "Max fancies himself in lust with me, and evidently isn't hampered by your scruples. Your younger brother isn't one to give up easily."

Daniel looked ready to explode. His neck turned red, his frown became fearsome, and he stalked away. He stood with his back to her for long moments. But when he faced her again, his expression was controlled. He pulled off his glasses and polished them on his sleeve. "Max has a little maturing to do yet. He'll gain a finer sense of judgment with age, I'm sure."

"Ouch." She feigned a grimace. "Going for the jugular now, are you? And here I am, a lady in distress, without the means to fight you." She batted her eyes at him, just to make certain he'd caught her double entendre.

Daniel frowned at her, then spoke to the nurse. "Fill

out the dog-bite card, then get Ms. McGee some scrubs and help her into them. I'll pull my car around to the front.''

Lace would have kicked him if she was sure she wouldn't hurt herself. ''I haven't agreed to go with you, you know.''

He never paused on his way out the door. ''I don't recall asking you.''

She sighed. Now she was in for it. Even her taunting hadn't turned him away, as it usually did. Why would Daniel do such a thing? It unnerved her, but then, the man himself unnerved her. Still, she liked the way he polished his glasses, the way he held his shoulders so straight. Actually, on some basic, primal level, she liked a lot of things about him.

Too bad he was such a rotten chauvinistic jerk.

Two

"**Y**our car smells like you, Daniel. All spicy and manly and—" she drew a deep breath "*—nice.*"

Daniel had to use all his concentration to keep them on the road. Ever since he'd settled Lace—very gently—into his back seat, she'd been hitting him with little comments like that. They were getting tougher to ignore. His touted self-control held only by a ragged thread.

He glanced into the rearview mirror and saw her resting on her side, managing to look elegant and sexy in a pair of worn scrubs with her black cloak tossed over her like a blanket. The blue color of the scrubs seemed out of place on her. Lace wore black almost without exception. She did it for effect, he was certain, and he had to admit, she always looked striking. The contrast of her pale blond hair and bright green eyes against the black made a very enticing picture.

But then, she'd look every bit as enticing with no clothes on at all.

He chased that errant thought right out of his mind and cleared his throat with difficulty. ''That's the leather you smell. My car may be sensible, but it's also top of the line.''

''Like you, Daniel?''

He managed a scoffing sound. Damn her, why wouldn't she let up on him? Usually her little barbs and sexual innuendos were well timed, not issued with the rapid-fire succession of a submachine gun blast. He tried to change the subject. ''How're you feeling? You holding up okay?''

''Don't worry about me, you'll give me a stroke. It's not what I'm used to from you. The shock could well kill me.''

''Lace…''

''I'm fine. Just a little drowsy.''

She sounded drowsy, sexy and slumberous, and his undisciplined mind supplied erotic images of her first waking in the morning after a long night of lovemaking. He had to grind his teeth together. With a slightly deeper tone to his voice, he said, ''I'll have you home and settled in soon. You're in pain and you need to rest.''

With a little sigh, she shifted and he again looked in the rearview mirror. She tried to hide her discomfort from him and that angered him. He didn't want her to be stoic, didn't want her consideration. He wanted to relish his dislike of her, to think only on what he knew was right and true about her.

He'd written her a prescription for pain pills, but now it struck him that she had no way to get them. He and Annie no longer discussed her, since it seemed a bone of contention, but he knew enough about her to know she was alone here in Ohio, with no family close by to lend her a hand. She couldn't very well go after the prescription herself, and with Max and Annie unavailable, she might not have anyone she could call if she needed help. The next few days would be rough for her.

For now, at least, she needed him.

Just that quickly he decided to fetch the pills for her to make certain she was able to settle comfortably. He was off tomorrow, and he had nothing more important planned than his own gift shopping to do. With Christmas only two weeks away, he was running out of time. But he could spare a day or two for Lace. After all, his male intellect reasoned, his sister thought of Lace as family. And though they were at odds a lot more these days thanks to Lace's interference, he cared a great deal about his sister.

Daniel pulled into the lot in front of her apartment building and turned off the car. Once before he'd been here, to pick up Annie when her car had died. Though he hadn't gone inside, his brain had memorized everything about the location of Lace's home. He knew which apartment was hers on the second landing, and now he realized there was a long flight of steps inside.

He looked over the seat at Lace while she shoved herself more or less upright, balancing on her uninjured hip. The effort caused her to pale and grimace in pain and he silently cursed her stubbornness even as he ordered, "Sit still, Lace. I'll carry you up."

He heard her strained laughter as he got out of the car, but it didn't matter. He'd made up his mind, and he knew his duty, repugnant as it might be. He shook his head at himself. Touching Lace wouldn't be the least bit displeasing. He didn't like her, but he wasn't dead, and as a man, he was more than a little aware of her allure.

When he opened her door, his intent obvious, she gave him a wary look and said, "Daniel, really, this isn't... Don't you dare! *Put me down!*"

He didn't give her a chance to argue with him. He tightened his hold and carefully scooped her up, making certain to keep his arms high on her back and low on her thighs so he wouldn't add to her pain. He hefted her out of the car while she made a loud and furious ruckus.

"Good grief, are you nuts?" She gasped and sputtered and tried to twist away. "What will my neighbors say?"

"I don't give a damn what they say." He bumped the car door shut with his hip, jarring her slightly.

Lace made a small sound, then wrapped her arms around his neck and held on, her grip almost painful. "You're being totally ridiculous, Daniel."

"If you'd stop clucking and carrying on, no one will even notice we're here. Quiet down and hold still before you hurt yourself."

They entered the building—and ran into three neighbors. Lace hid her face in his neck. Soft hair brushed his cheek and he couldn't help but breathe in her musky feminine scent. She felt warm and sweet and...right in his arms. Her plump rounded breasts pressed into his ribs and her thighs felt womanly soft draped over his arm. Damn, but he would not allow his physical attraction to her to override his common sense.

He stared at all three people, daring any of them to ask.

One man stepped forward, twisting his hands together. "Is she all right? Lace, honey, how bad was it?"

The dog owner, Daniel decided, and his scowl deepened. The man appeared to be in his mid-forties, had at least three thick gold chains around his neck, and obviously enjoyed lifting weights. Daniel tightened his hold possessively—not that *he* was possessive. ''She got close to a hundred stitches. The dog was reported, of course.''

Lace bit his ear. He almost dropped her he was so surprised. It wasn't that it had hurt, because she'd only given him a small nip, but it had nearly buckled his knees. The feel of her open mouth on his skin, the touch of her sharp little teeth, her warm breath, had felt very like a lover's nibble, and suddenly every male hormone he possessed screamed an alert. It took every ounce of his flagging control to keep his expression impassive.

Lace leaned away from him, sending a smile to the other man. ''Hello, Frank. I'm going to be fine, so you can stop worrying. And I've decided not to press charges this time. But I will have to insist that you check into some training for him. He can't just go around losing control like that. And from now on, make certain he's kept on a leash.''

Relief spread over Frank's face, despite her stern tone. He appeared ready to fall at Lace's feet in gratitude. ''I'd already decided the very same thing, Lace, honey. And I really am sorry. I swear I won't let him loose again, now that I know there's a problem. I just don't know what got into him.''

''The cat that tried to use me as a shield enticed him beyond his endurance, I'm sure.''

''I know he was after the cat, but he's never so much as even growled at a person before.''

Lace reached out to pat his shoulder, leaving it to Daniel to balance her weight. ''I'll be fine, Frank, really. The important thing is to make certain it never happens again.''

Frank turned to the other two men, both older, but still not *old*. ''We've been talking, and if there's any-

thing you need, just let one of us know. We'll be glad
to help you out while you recuperate.''

Daniel finally found his voice. Here was the perfect
solution, a way for him to leave her, in familiar hands,
so he could go home and retire after his long day. He
opened his mouth and said, ''That won't be necessary.
I'll take care of her.''

Silence fell. Daniel heard the words, knew he'd said
them himself, and almost shook his head to deny it anyway. He didn't want to take care of Lace. Good grief,
he didn't even like the woman. He vigorously *disliked*
her! He disapproved of her and her immoderate effect
on him. He racked his brain for a tactful way out of the
predicament he'd just put himself in when Lace leaned
back to see his face.

She looked shocked and ready to protest, which irritated him even more. Perversely, he decided he *would*
hang around and there was no way she could stop him.
''Not a word out of you, lady. And if you're done so-
cializing, I'd like to get to your place. You're not heavy,
but then, you're no featherweight, either.''

The men scrambled away, saying hasty good-nights
as Daniel started up the stairs. Lace grinned and rubbed
her fingertips over his nape. He felt the caress all the
way to his suddenly tight abdomen.

''Putting a strain on your back, am I?''

''No more than you strain my patience,'' he muttered,
and added, ''All that male adoration piled on your beautiful head was enough to make me ill. Now I know why
you chose this apartment. Are there any females in res-
idence at all?''

Lace cupped his cheek, forcing him to look at her.
''Beautiful head? By any chance, was that an actual
compliment I just heard, Daniel?''

His foot paused on the next step and he blinked at her. Her smile teased him and her fingertips were gentle on his jaw. His glasses slipped down his nose a fraction of an inch.

"I didn't mean it," he growled, then stomped the rest of the way up the staircase. When they reached her door, he asked, "Where are your keys?"

"In my cloak pocket. Just a minute." She fished them out, then leaned over and unlocked the door. She didn't turn the doorknob or open it, however. "Thank you for seeing me home, Daniel. I appreciate it. Now when your sister sings your praises, I suppose I'll have to agree just a bit—on rare and specific occasions."

She smiled at him, and Daniel only stared back. Irritating female. "Open the door, Lace."

Her brow puckered and her look became wary. "You can put me down now. I'm perfectly capable of walking in on my own steam."

"Open the door. I've gotten you this far, I might as well see it through. Besides, you'll need some help getting settled."

"Oh? And do you escort all your patients home from the hospital and give them personal assistance?"

It was a strain, but he managed to keep his tone even. He would not let her provoke him. "Only the ones who ingratiate themselves on my family. Annie would never forgive me if I left you to fend for yourself. Now, open the door."

"I don't want you in my apartment."

She'd looked down when she said that, and suspicions grew in rapid succession. He imagined mirrors on the ceilings, sex manuals strewn about, maybe a man or two tucked into the corners awaiting her direction. For some reason, his temper simmered and he reached past her for the doorknob.

"Dammit, Daniel, this is my home and you're not invited in!"

"Hush, Lace."

"That's a reoccurring tune with you, isn't it? Any time I inject a little reason into this bizarre situation, you tell me to hush."

She stiffened in his arms as he stepped inside—and stopped. This was not the home he'd envisioned for Lace McGee—love expert, sex guru, relationship connoisseur. There wasn't a single black item to be seen, no obvious suggestive reading material, nothing to indicate the woman he knew—the woman he held in his arms— might abide here.

This looked like a grandmother's retreat. Doilies covered every surface of the battered antique tables, and Tiffany lamps sent soft glows of color everywhere. The couch was overstuffed, brightly floral, soft. Handwoven rag rugs decorated polished hardwood floors.

Daniel stared and then stared some more. For the moment, he forgot he held Lace. "I've just stepped out of the tornado and into Oz."

She squirmed in his arms. "Shut up, Daniel, and put me down."

She startled him out of his study. Slowly, he let her slip down his body, his gaze on her face. Her cheeks flushed and her beautiful green eyes avoided his. He held her carefully until she'd gained her balance, favoring her injured side. "Does your mother or some distant aunt live here with you, Lace?"

"I don't have a distant aunt."

"Lace?"

"Of course not." She still wouldn't look at him,

which irked his temper again. First she baited him with endless sexual innuendos, and now she played shy.

"Then who decorated this place?"

She hit his shoulder with a small fist. "I did, you idiot. And there's nothing wrong with my home, so stop gawking."

She turned away and started—with an awkward hobbling gait—down the hall. Daniel looked around once more, and followed her. "But there's so much...color."

"Yeah, so? I enjoy color."

She sounded her most belligerent, and he frowned. "No, you don't. You like black. You always wear black. Your car is black. Even your luggage is black, for crying out loud. I bet your panties are even black, though I couldn't tell since they were covered with so much blood."

She glared over her shoulder, sending him a look of acute dislike, then tried to stalk into her bedroom. But with her recent injury, the effect was minimal. The numbing would have worn off by now, and it had to hurt like the very devil. Daniel followed her, thinking to explain that he'd go get her pain pills. He walked into her bedroom and stopped cold in his tracks. No, it couldn't be. If the living room had been a surprise, this was enough to jump-start his heart.

At least a dozen small velvet pillows in a variety of soft muted hues were tossed atop a candy-striped bedspread with a dark pink dust ruffle. The sheer gauzy material that served as window coverings in a variety of pastel shades flowed across the glass in no particular order. He could easily imagine the room bathed in a pastel-hued rainbow whenever the sunlight shone through.

She wasn't the neatest of people. There were

clothes—all black—strewed over a rocker and the end of the bed. And peeking out from the under the bed... Daniel bent to pick up the gleaming material, then held it in the air. Panties. Tiny, shimmering, lime green panties that probably weighed no more than half an ounce. He tried to imagine her in them—and managed only too well.

Lace snatched the panties out of his hand with a low growl. "Okay, Daniel. I'm home. I'm settled. I'm going to change clothes and go to bed and try to forget about big-jawed dogs and arrogant pushy doctors. You can leave now. Your *duty* is complete."

"You wear lime green underwear?"

"Oh, for Pete's sake!" She looked apoplectic. "What do you care what color underwear I wear?"

His brows pulled down tight enough to give him a headache. Confusion swirled, his world tilted. And it was all her fault, the little witch. Why did she keep doing this to him? "I don't understand, Lace."

She huffed out a breath and glared up at him. He stared right back. He was bigger, so therefore it stood to reason he could be twice as stubborn. Finally she gave up. "I'm horrible at matching stuff up, okay? Look around. It's like a circus on the Fourth of July in here. But I *love* color, I really do. All colors, every shade, deep and sinful, light and playful. I need color. It's just that I could never get the knack of putting clothes together, and since I have to appear in public a lot, I just decided it was easier to stick to simple basic black. That way, when I'm in a hurry, I can pick out my outfit without worrying whether or not I'll match or be put together properly."

"You wear black because you have no fashion sense?" His poor suspicious brain couldn't quite assimilate all these new notions, not when they went against everything he thought he knew about her. "It isn't because it's dramatic and adds a special effect to your blond hair and green eyes?"

Slowly, her most provocative smile appeared and she looked at him through her lashes. "Why, Daniel. You've noticed my eyes? And my hair? Was that another compliment, by any chance?"

He took two steps back and his jaw clenched. "I didn't mean it." She continued to grin and he sought a safer topic. "I'm going to run out and get your prescriptions while you get settled in bed. No pajamas."

"Are you suggesting I sleep naked?"

His hands shook and he wanted to smack her for planting that sizzling mental picture firmly into his beleaguered mind. "Put on a gown." His gaze went to the panties she still held. They looked like a bright neon beacon, calling to him, and he added, "Forget underwear. It'll only irritate your wound."

"I never sleep in underwear."

His heart tripped against his ribs and he felt her purring tone clear to his groin. With strong resolution, he kept his gaze on her face. "Do you need any help, Lace?"

"I can manage. But take the spare key off the wall in the kitchen. That way you can let yourself back in. I'll just get myself settled in bed—to wait for you."

Damn her, she was really enjoying herself now. He should just leave. She deserved a little discomfort. Eventually someone would get the medicine for her, and she could get her jollies torturing some other poor male instead of him.

But he couldn't do it. Lace needed him, curse her headstrong, sexy hide, and he told himself his decision

to look after her had nothing to do with any personal
lust for her. It was just that he was used to protecting
and caring for others. It had become a habit, started the
day his mother was buried and his father made it clear
he couldn't overcome his own grief, much less that of
his children. Someone had needed to hug his little sister
at night when she cried. And someone had needed to
reassure his brother Max when he'd become so withdrawn and sullen.

Annie and Max had needed him then. They needed
him still. They looked to him for guidance, almost as a
father figure, and Daniel knew they cared about Lace as
a friend. He was a doctor, and the patriarch of the family
despite his father's flighty presence. It was his duty to
see Lace situated as comfortably as possible.

His reasoning sounded lame even to his own ears, but
he wasn't about to delve any further for motivation.
Therein lay personal disaster and he knew it. He took
one more glance around at Lace's bedroom, then
stormed out, overcome by mixed feelings. This was either the worst idea he'd ever had—*or the best.*

"I found an old black T-shirt to sleep in so I wouldn't
further lacerate your expectations of my wardrobe."

Lace waited for some response, but Daniel only nodded. He'd been withdrawn and almost wary since returning a few minutes ago. Very unlike his usual con-
frontational self. His cheeks were ruddy from the cold,
and his dark hair was mussed from the wind. He pulled
his glasses off and polished them on his sleeve, removing a few snowflakes. She enjoyed the sight of his light
brown, thickly lashed eyes, how intense they could be,
how serious. He slid the glasses back onto his straight
nose and went to get a glass of water from her kitchen.

Lace kept the bedspread pulled up to her throat. She was on her back, with a pillow propped beneath her leg on her injured side; she felt vulnerable with Daniel there, aware of her awkward discomfort. But when Daniel leaned down to hand her the pill and the water she noticed how rigid he looked, and it annoyed her. He always acted as if he expected her to sexually accost his poor male body at any given moment—and like he'd hate it. Unaccountable prude.

Pain pulled at her, but still she managed a small taunting smile, knowing how he'd react to it. She made a point of letting her fingertips graze his palm as she took the pill from him, and rather than hold the glass herself, she held his wrist, which forced him to tilt the glass to her lips.

He stared at her mouth and his nostrils flared. The hypocrite. He might disdain her supposed lack of morals, but he fantasized the same as she did. It was men like him that kept her profession thriving. His antiquated notions of what was right for a woman, in comparison to the acceptable standards for a man, made her furious. At least half her calls at the radio station dealt with issues over the double standard of sexual freedom for men and women.

She gave him a sloe-eyed look and smiled. ''Mmm. Thank you, Daniel.''

''You're welcome.''

He sounded like a frog, and Lace had to bite back her satisfied chuckle. ''I never noticed before what big hands you have.'' She pretended to study his hand—then came to the realization he really did have big hands. His fingers were long and blunt and smooth. A doctor's capable hands. She shivered with a newly awakened awareness.

"Are you cold?" As he asked, Daniel pulled away from her. "I could get you another blanket."

"I'm fine. Will the pill make me sleepy?"

"Probably." His gaze darted around her room again. He kept looking at everything, and every time he ended up shaking his head.

His disapproval was obvious, and she should have been used to it by now. In her mind, there were two major groups of men. Those who wanted to take advantage of her *expertise,* and those who discounted her expertise as ludicrous simply because she was a young woman. Her mother had always had a similar problem with men who wanted her only for her money and men who thought her money would never buy her any class. Still, her mother had kept trying. Lace had no intention of making that same mistake.

She understood Daniel and his attitudes. By her own design, she courted his disdain. She used it as her defense against him, and Annie had backed her up, respecting her wishes to present herself in any light she chose as long as she didn't have to lie to Daniel. But since Daniel never bothered to ask for the truth, Annie could leave him to his ridiculous beliefs. Daniel would never really know her. And that fact made her a little sad, because she loved Annie. She was the closest friend Lace had ever had. Even Max was okay once you got a handle on him and his robust disregard for propriety. The middle brother did like to shake people up, most especially his big brother. Lace rather liked that about Max. It gave them something in common.

But Daniel... He continued to look around her room, his expression almost comical in its fascinated study. "I didn't leave any other unmentionables laying about."

He turned back to her, shaken from his engrossed examination of her room. "What?"

"If you're really that curious, I keep my panties in the third drawer of the bureau." She waved in that direction. "Feel free."

A red flush stained his neck and his brows snapped down. "You really don't possess a single ounce of decorum, do you?"

"Me?" She'd gotten her desired result, but now her own temper ignited. It was very late, she was tired, and it had been an eventful day. "You're the one who keeps gawking! You're the one who forced yourself into my home and picked up my underwear and keeps looking around like Sherlock Holmes trying to find some wicked evidence of my sordid love life."

He seemed stunned by her outburst—but no more so than she. Generally, she was even-tempered and almost never raised her voice. She'd honed the knack of cutting obnoxious men down with a single sneer or a well-chosen phrase. Daniel, however, tended to bring out the worst in her. She scowled at him, then grumbled, "I'm sorry."

Daniel shook his head, his gaze glued to her face, probing and serious. "No, it was my fault. I didn't mean to make you uncomfortable, and I certainly didn't mean to…gawk. It's just that I never expected…"

"I know. You thought I hated color."

He pulled up a chair and sat beside the bed. "I like your apartment, Lace. It's pretty."

"And colorful."

He laughed. "Well, yeah, but in a nice way."

She studied his handsome face in some surprise. It was the first time she could ever recall him laughing with her. "I like the way you laugh, Daniel. You should do it more often. Annie assures me you're a happy fellow, but you always seem so staid around me.''

At first he looked defensive, and then he sighed. ''I suppose I am overly serious at times. But then, that's the life of a doctor, especially in the emergency room. There's not a lot of time left for goofing off.''

Lace thought about Daniel's life. He hadn't had an easy childhood, not with his mother dying when he was so young. Annie said he'd decided to become a doctor then. According to Annie, Daniel had been twelve years old when he'd sworn he'd learn how to save people. Perhaps that was enough to take the gaiety out of anyone's life.

Her own mother had never had it easy, and her vulnerability had added to her troubles, especially when it came to relationships. But at least she'd grown up with a mother, and she and Lace had enjoyed a unique life together. Not always a happy one, but it had its special moments.

On impulse, Lace reached out and took Daniel's hand. It felt warm and strong, and she sighed. ''I don't make it very easy on you, do I?''

He looked down at their clasped hands for a moment, his expression very contemplative as his fingers curled around hers. ''You like to make me a little crazy, I think.''

''Actually, I love it.'' She grinned, feeling almost drunk from the pain medicine and a little too relaxed. ''You're so easy to provoke.''

''So you love color and you love tormenting me. What else do you love, Lace?''

He was very serious now. Lace realized that for the first time, in some very minute way, he was actually trying to get to know her. Caution warred with the need to share herself, to erase the misconceptions between them. But she didn't dare. Regardless of what she said to him, they'd never see things the same way. They were simply too different.

She settled on keeping things light. It wouldn't be safe to share herself with a man like Daniel. He'd always disapprove of her, and she couldn't get involved with a man who didn't trust and understand her. She shrugged. "I love little children, their honesty and their laughter and their chubby pink cheeks. And I love commercials. They're much better than most television programs."

"Baby cheeks and commercials, huh?"

She could hear the laughter in his tone and she smiled. "I love sunshine and swimming, but also the purity of a first snow. I love talking with people and maybe sometimes helping them. I love thick cotton socks that keep my feet warm on a cold day, and sheets fresh from the laundry, and warm spring breezes. And most of all, I love Christmas carols."

Daniel tightened his hand on hers and looked…disturbed. His tone was very low and deep when he spoke. "I like Christmas carols, too. My mom used to start singing them in mid-October and kept it up till the New Year. I have just about every Christmas CD ever produced."

"Do you sing along with them?"

"When there's no one around to be offended by my less than sterling voice."

"Me, too. At the top of my lungs."

His thumb rubbed over her knuckles, then he said softly, "You don't have a Christmas tree."

Uh-oh. Just that quickly they left the lighthearted stuff and entered into the emotional. She pulled her hand away, using the excuse of smoothing her blankets. Her

head felt muddled with fatigue and medicine and the
newness of speaking so casually with Daniel. It was dark
outside with only a little moonlight coming through her
rainbow-sheathed window. Quiet surrounded them, his
expression was intent. And he'd seen her bare backside.
Suddenly things seemed far too intimate.

Without looking at him, she said, "A tree seems like
a lot of fuss and bother for just me." She hoped she
sounded casual, not maudlin. Christmas was a hard time
for a person alone, but she didn't want him to know it.
Regardless of this moment, they didn't like each other,
and she couldn't give him future ammunition to use
against her.

"You don't entertain on the holidays? You don't have
any family to visit with you?"

"My mother lives in Florida but she travels over the
holidays, visiting all her…friends." The reality of that
hurt, and she closed her eyes to hide her emotions from
him. The medicine pulled at her, numbing her wits, and
she heard herself whisper, "I know you won't believe
it, but I really don't entertain all that often. I'm not much
of a partying person."

He didn't say a word, and she finally opened her eyes
to meet his gaze, though forcing her lids to lift wasn't
easy. Rather than seeing the disbelief she expected, he
looked thoughtful. "Daniel?"

His name sounded slurred, and she frowned. Daniel
reached out and smoothed a lock of hair away from her
temple. The tender touch sent her pulse rioting. Her head
pounded, her stomach felt jumpy.

A reaction to the pain pills, she decided. She never
did react well to medication.

"Go to sleep, Lace. Just give in to the pills and relax.
Everything's going to be okay."

She didn't understand that cryptic comment, but her awareness was fading without her permission.

Her eyes closed and her body seemed to sigh into the mattress. She heard Daniel say softly, ''If you need anything, I'll be here.''

''Here?'' The word emerged as a mere whisper, barely heard by her own ears.

''I'm staying the night, Lace.'' His fingers touched her cheek, her chin. ''I don't want to leave you alone.''

She struggled to open her eyes again, to get her mouth to work. She didn't want him in her apartment all night, didn't want to be indebted to him. Most of all, she didn't want to be vulnerable, to have him watch her in her sleep, explore her home without her awareness. But it was too late.

She fell asleep with his promise still in her ears and his large strong hand holding her own.

And surprisingly, she felt comforted by his presence.

Three

The soreness went bone deep, tugging at her, making her temples pound. It hadn't been a restful night, despite the pain medication, but Daniel had done his best to assist her. Maybe that was the problem: Daniel.

Throughout the night, whenever she'd so much as move, Daniel would suddenly be there, at her bedside, tending her, speaking to her in soft, soothing tones. So unlike the Daniel she knew. *So tempting.*

Walking was a definite chore this morning. Even her back and hips hurt. Probably from the awkward way she'd positioned herself in the bed. She found a robe, a pale pink, soft cotton piece of nonsense that fueled her sense of whimsy and completely hid her black T-shirt. She stared at it, wondering if the soft color or the sweet ruffles would lacerate Daniel's sensibilities. He did seem to have a thing about mixing her with color.

Shrugging, she slipped it on and tied the belt tightly.

After brushing her teeth and washing her face, she made her way cautiously to the kitchen to start the coffee.

On her way past the living room she heard a soft snore and froze. No man had ever slept in her apartment; no man had ever even *been* in her apartment. How it made her feel now, to have Daniel snoring on her couch, couldn't quite be measured, not first thing in the morning, without coffee and with too little sleep.

Investigating, she inched farther into the darkened living room, following the low sound of deep male breathing until she stood beside the short, fat couch. Daniel, overflowing the squat piece of furniture at every angle, lay on his back, his shirt gone, his belt removed and his pants unbuttoned. His bare feet, long and narrow and sexy really, when she took the time to look at them, hung over the opposite arm of the couch. His face was turned slightly toward her, his lips parted, his silky brown hair mussed and falling over his forehead. Beard shadow darkened his face and his thick, gorgeous lashes rested on his high cheekbones.

She forgot her pain. She forgot her coffee.

He had a lot of soft-looking, light brown hair on his chest; she liked that. His shoulders were hard, the flesh pulled smooth and taut over bone and sinew and muscle. With one arm propped behind his head, she could see the flex of his biceps, the thickness of his forearm, his obvious strength.

But she'd always known he was strong, at least, in the most important ways. He'd cared for his family when no else would or could, and continued to care for them, even now when they were all grown. He handled crises at the hospital every day in his sure, confident manner. He had conviction and determination down to a fine art. She admired him, even though she didn't want to.

Seeing his physical strength now shouldn't do this to her, shouldn't make her heart flutter, or her stomach curl tight. But it did. She looked from his chest to his flat belly, not ridged with muscles, just lean and firm and manly. Through the open clasp of his pants she could see the start of a dark, silky line of hair, the elastic of white briefs, and below that... She inhaled thickly through her nose.

"Good morning."

Startled, she jerked her gaze to a more appropriate place, like his face, and then from embarrassment because he watched her so intently, to the kitchen. "I was going to start some coffee."

He didn't move and his voice stayed deep and lazy, amused. "You were looking at me."

"You snore."

Chuckling, he rubbed his face and stretched like a big, confident cat, and once again her gaze roamed over him. His dress slacks were badly wrinkled and without his glasses, he looked... She liked his glasses, but he looked softer without them, not as stern. It unnerved her.

He sat up and she noticed the flex and roll of muscles in his chest and shoulders. He yawned hugely, with no sense of his polite, restrained manner, and then grinned at her. "This couch makes a terrible bed."

"Maybe that's because it was never meant to be a bed."

"After last night, I can understand why." He stood, and when she didn't back up, their toes almost touched. Reaching out, he tucked a wayward tress of hair behind her ear and stroked her cheek. "Did you finally get any sleep?"

She could smell him, a deep, dark, musky male scent that was delicious and enticing and forbidden. Why was he being so nice all of a sudden? Was this part of his solicitous doctor mode? Somehow, she didn't think so.

"I slept fine." Her voice sounded like a croak.

"Liar." He took her shoulders and moved her gently aside. "You shouldn't even be out of bed. You should have awakened me if you wanted coffee. That's what I'm here for." He urged her toward the cushions he'd just vacated. "Lie down and I'll get you a pillow."

She started to protest, but he still held her, and never in her life had she felt so tongue-tied. "Daniel..."

"Shh. How do you like your coffee?" He lifted her legs carefully up onto the couch, putting a soft cushion beneath her, situating her as if she had no strength or will at all. "Strong, I hope. I need the caffeine."

So did she. The damned couch was still warm from his body, and on it, his scent was strong, stirring her, making her think ridiculous things. The urge to reach up and pull him down with her was so acute, she had to resort to sarcasm to save herself. "I'm not an invalid, and you're not my great-aunt, so you can stop the coddling. I'm fine."

He scratched his belly, distracting her once again, before slipping on his glasses. He finger-combed his hair, and Lace watched the silky strands glide in and out of his fingers. "You're not fine. I want you to take it easy—*very easy*—for at least forty-eight hours. After that, we'll see."

"You may be used to bossing Annie and Max around, but you're not my brother."

"Not your aunt, not your brother." He touched the tip of her nose without smiling, his expression intent. "Believe me, I've never felt remotely brotherly toward you."

He turned his back on her and went into the kitchen.

Lace heard the running of water, the clink of the glass carafe, the opening and closing of a cabinet. She sighed and flopped her head back to stare at the ceiling. How strange it seemed to have Daniel Sawyers in her kitchen. Beyond strange, it seemed bizarre, improbable, ridiculous. Maybe she was imagining the whole thing. Maybe…

"I'm going to take a quick shower. Sit tight. I'll be done before the coffee is."

Her eyes widened and her face felt stiff. Daniel in her shower? Naked? She'd never be able to use that shower again without wicked images invading her mind. How unfair of him to shove his way in, to dominate her thoughts and take over her home.

Used to taking care of herself, she wasn't about to let him run her life. She waited until she heard the shower start, then limped her way into the kitchen. Pain or not, she refused to be a burden, and she refused to allow Daniel to get one up on her. Who knew when he might use this damned weakness against her?

She found a refrigerated package of cinnamon rolls and put them in the oven. The coffee was almost done so she got out two large mugs, spoons, sugar, cream.

"What the hell are you doing?"

She jumped, almost dropping the napkins and jarring her leg enough that she winced in pain. Daniel, his wet hair brushed back from his forehead, his chest still damp, his lashes spiky, stood in her kitchen scowling at her. For some insane reason, she almost felt guilty. She simply couldn't reconcile this scenario with reality. No man had ever stood half-naked in her kitchen after his shower, but she could have imagined almost any other man in such a position easier than she could Daniel.

He saw her grimace of pain and moved toward her,

slipping his arm around her waist. The dampness of his skin, the warmth of his bare chest, caused her to stiffen even more.

"Do you need me to carry you?"

She needed him to go away so she could stop acting like an idiot. "No. Don't touch me."

He laughed. "This show of shyness from Lace the Sex Expert? Lace the Uninhibited?"

Her head snapped around and she glared. "This show of concern from Daniel the Ice Man? Daniel the Discreet?"

The barest trace of regret clouded his eyes before he released her, his expression impassive. They stood that way for long moments, each watching the other, until finally Daniel sighed. "I understand how you might feel, Lace. I really do. I know you despise me. But right now, there are other factors involved. One, I'm a doctor, your doctor, and I'm telling you that you have to take it easy. That means staying off your feet and keeping as much stress off the injury as you can. Two, you're my little sister's best friend. I can't ignore that. Annie would have a fit if I just left you alone right now. And three, we're both adults. Surely you can behave like one."

Lace narrowed her eyes and tucked in her chin. An impressive repertoire of scathing comments, one right after the other, tripped to the tip of her tongue. She opened her mouth to blast him with her cold disdain, her well-rehearsed verses reserved for obnoxious men, and said, "I don't despise you."

He blinked twice, rapidly. She imagined she looked just as surprised. That was not what she'd intended to say. Not at all.

Daniel narrowed his eyes and rolled in his lips, his brow drawn. "Then…"

"I have things I have to do, Daniel." Escape seemed her only viable option now. "Mail to read and answer. A show to prepare. Appointments."

"You can't go out. No, Lace, don't go all stiff-faced on me. As a doctor, I'm telling you that you have to take it easy. It's icy outside. If you slip and fall, there's no telling what damage you'll add to your wound. And that's in addition to the harm you'll cause just by trudging through the snow and frigid wind. As far as your mail, I can bring it to you in bed. I have a lap-top computer you can use if you'd like."

She hesitated and he seemed to explode. "Dammit, don't be an idiot! Your health is at stake here."

She slumped. "I have phone calls to make, my laundry to do…"

"I'll help you."

The laughter erupted and she clapped a hand over her mouth, then peeked up at him. "I beg your pardon?"

A red flush started at his neck and worked its way to his ears. "I'm off today. I'll run home and get a change of clothes, my lap-top, and I'll pick up your mail and something for us to eat later for lunch. While you make your phone calls, I'll go downstairs and throw in some of your laundry."

She fanned her face, pretending a near swoon. "I think I need to sit down."

"No sitting. Come here. And don't shy away from me like that. Just pretend I'm one of your admirers." He hesitated. "Or lovers."

"Ha! I'm not quite that creative." She didn't add that imagining any lover was well beyond her capability.

Grinning, he said, "I know. It does stretch the boundaries of inspiration, doesn't it?" He took her arm and once again led her to the sofa. "Lie down. *Stay* down."

"I'm not a disobedient pet."

"No pet would dare be this disobedient or I'd take it to the pound. Now, I'm going to get you a few more pillows and if you need anything else, please, ask me."

Her head swam. She tried to reconcile why Daniel would be doing all this, why he'd willingly give up his day off to hang around and pester her. No logical reasons presented themselves to her bedeviled brain.

He came back and slipped one of her lemon yellow pillows under her head, another under her leg. "How's that? Are you comfortable?"

Unable to meet his gaze, she nodded. She'd never in her entire life had anyone pamper her. The feeling was unsettling, to say the least. "Thank you."

"Lace."

Lace lifted her gaze to his, confused, nervous, words beyond her. With him still leaning close, one hand on the back of the couch, the other on the cushion, they stared at each other. For long seconds their gazes held, and Daniel slowly, almost imperceptibly, leaned closer. His attention moved to her mouth. Lace parted her lips to take in a deep breath, allowing some necessary oxygen to reach her brain, and got stung by reality.

"I smell something burning."

Daniel paused. "Hmm?"

Oh, that low husky rumble. Lace realized now how dangerous this whole situation had become. Somehow in the space of a single night their antagonism had mutated into something much more elemental between men and women, something she'd never thought to deal with. Something she suspected had been there all along.

She cleared her throat. "I put rolls in the oven. They're burning."

Daniel jerked back, and with understanding came a

look of appalled fascination. Lace continued to stare. She felt as though she couldn't quite breathe, as if the world had gone totally hazy. She knew better, had learned early on the ramifications of making such a horrible, ridiculous mistake. But she couldn't deny it any longer. As ill suited as they were, as much as he annoyed her and as much as she enjoyed annoying him, she lusted after Daniel Sawyers.

It was probably the fault of her new revelation that she didn't pay any attention when Daniel went to retrieve the rolls. He asked, his voice only slightly gruff, how she liked her coffee and she answered him, without thought, that she wanted it sweetened and with cream. He carried the cup to her, along with the rolls, already iced. They ate in a kind of unsettled, stunned silence.

Whatever intimacy had existed a minute ago was gone now, replaced by propriety and common sense and belated panic. Lace sipped her hot coffee and reminded herself of all the relationships that had gotten started on such a shaky foundation as lust, relationships she helped to redefine as part of her profession. She remembered all the emotional pain her mother had put herself through, trying to build on something as insubstantial as physical need. She thought of Daniel's cursed opinion of her.

And still, she wanted him.

"You're in pain again, aren't you?"

Her thoughts disrupted, Lace looked at him and shrugged. "A little." Actually more than a little. The dull throbbing discomfort in her backside had increased to the point that she didn't want to move, because moving caused a definite sharp pinch of pain.

"You need to take another pain pill."

She hated to admit he was right, but she didn't relish playing the role of the martyr, either. She started to rise, but he halted her. "I'll get it, and then I've got to get going. Promise me you'll take it easy until I get back."

So he planned to just ignore the preceding moments of passion? That figured. "You're sure you don't mind doing this?"

"I believe I was rather insistent."

"All right. Suit yourself. It's not often a girl gets to be treated like a queen. Maybe I can even find a small bell somewhere that I can ring when I want you. I'll just pretend you're my erstwhile slave, awaiting my meanest direction. What do you think?"

"I think you're pushing your luck."

Lace chuckled. "Just teasing. I'll be a good queen and rest here while I make my phone calls. That should take me at least an hour."

He brought the phone, her phone book, some of the correspondence that required a personal call, and a pen and paper to her. Lace wouldn't have been surprised if he'd set a glass and water pitcher beside her, he seemed so diligent in his efforts to please.

He turned to her as he shrugged into his shirt. She found the process fascinating. Men did things differently, moved differently, even breathed differently. Seeing Daniel in the act of something as mundane as dressing proved fascinating when compared to how her own body moved while performing the same duty. She wished she could watch him shave, though he looked good, rugged, with whiskers on his lean cheeks.

"What do you like to eat? I'll pick something up for a late lunch."

"Mexican," she said without hesitation. "Something hot and spicy and with lots of sauce."

Daniel laughed. "At least that doesn't surprise me. Somehow I knew you'd be a spicy kind of woman."

Lace tilted her head and looked at him with lowered brows.

He pulled on his shoes, still grinning. "No offense, Lace. Just a joke."

"What about you? What will you eat?"

"Mexican is fine by me."

"Ha! Now that does surprise a body, doesn't it? I mean, I definitely *never* thought of you as a spicy kind of man."

He stood and slipped on his coat. On his way out the door, he stopped to look at her over his shoulder. "One of these days, I may just surprise you."

Lace felt her mouth fall open, but he was already gone, the door closing softly behind him.

"It all comes back to how you feel about the whole thing, Renee. If you like him playing the dominant role, if it satisfies you, then there's nothing in the world wrong with it."

Daniel froze one step inside the door. Lace glanced at him, waved a short hello, then gave her attention back to the phone. Dominant? What kind of conversation had he walked in on? *One typical for Lace,* he realized, disgusted with himself.

He closed the door behind him and set his load on the foyer table. Lace had a ton of mail, much more than he'd anticipated. He'd really had no idea she received so much correspondence through her profession, or that she'd become such a popular personality. Hanging his damp, snow frosted coat on the coat tree, he pretended not to listen to the conversation.

"I know it's 1998, and women are supposed to take a more active role, be more decisive and aggressive. But that's the whole thing, choices. What works for one woman, or for a couple, doesn't necessarily work for another. You don't want to let society standards restrict you, any more than you want your mate to. Only you know what feels good to you, what satisfies you. Don't worry about whether or not it's in the 'norm.' If you're comfortable with letting him dominate in your marriage, that's all that matters.''

His glasses fogged and he had to turn away. How was it every word out of Lace's mouth sounded like a purr of seduction? As if she said those things specifically to rile him, to arouse him? Irritated, especially given how soft he'd been feeling toward her when he'd left her apartment this morning, he stomped into the kitchen to put the Mexican food in the refrigerator. He'd made certain to have it packaged in a way that he could microwave it later and it would still taste fresh. He'd thought of her satisfaction at the banquet he'd compiled, the spicy enchiladas, the chili, the fajitas. He'd been so pleased with his efforts. Now he had his doubts.

Lace hadn't changed just because she'd been hurt. She wasn't suddenly vulnerable and needy just because she liked Christmas carols but had no one to share them with. She was still the same woman, the liberal who'd transformed his baby sister from tomboy to femme fatale. Her idea of entertainment was to harass him until his mind fogged with lust and his body reacted independently of his brain. He'd have to remember that.

Determined to provide the help he'd promised her, Daniel went in search of dirty laundry. He tried to ignore the ensuing discussion, but certain words jumped out at him, key words that told him all he needed to know about Lace McGee, sexual icon, vamp extraordinaire.

When he walked into her bedroom, he heard her voice

raise in a squeak on the phone. Seconds later, she came hobbling in behind him.

"What are you doing?"

He glanced up, pretending to be impervious to the way her pastel robe draped over her slim shoulders, to the way her moon-colored hair curled in disarray. How her bare feet looked pink and small and so very feminine. She stared back nervously, tucking her hair behind her ears and glancing around her room as if she suspected he might have stolen something.

"You're a slob. I was only picking up the laundry so I could go get it started."

Lace scowled. "I can pick up my own laundry."

"No, you need to take it easy." He reached for a T-shirt, then a lacy sock. She snatched them both out of his hands.

"Dammit, Daniel, I don't want you rifling through my things."

"Rifling? I hate to break it to you, Lace, but your dirty clothes aren't all that interesting to me."

"They were last night."

"Don't look so smug. Last night you took me by surprise. I expected your place to look…different. To reflect the woman you are."

Her back stiffened. "You don't have an inkling of the woman I am, so how could you possibly have had an accurate preconceived notion of my housing?"

He whistled through his teeth. "Wow. All that, huh?" She growled and he leaned back on her dresser. "What makes you think I don't know you?"

That stumped her. She opened her mouth twice, only to close it again.

"Well? Nothing to say?" She stubbornly shook her head and he knew he saw a measure of hurt on her features. It had to be physical. He refused to believe his opinion of her caused her a single moment of grief. "Dammit, will you lay down? Use the bed, that way you can watch me and you won't have to worry about me *rifling* through your things."

With her mouth tight and her expression rebellious, she did as he asked. Once she was settled on her side, she peered up at him and gave a sigh. "How come we're arguing again?"

"Damned if I know." Then he sighed, too. "Did you get your phone calls taken care of?"

"Most of them. That last one took longer than I thought. She was very upset."

"A disgruntled woman who's into bondage? Is that where your valuable time is dedicated these days?"

He knew even as he said it he wasn't being fair. It was just that she made him so confused with what he felt and what he ought to feel. How she spent her life shouldn't matter to him, but it did. He wanted her, more than he'd ever wanted any woman, and he knew he shouldn't. He didn't feel any real affection for her, much less the overpowering love people often spoke of. And he didn't believe in uninvolved sex. He'd had his share of sexual relationships, but he'd always liked the women and, more importantly, he'd respected them.

He thought about apologizing. Before he could even work up a good way to start, Lace burst out laughing. She laughed so hard, she fell onto her face on the mattress and he was left with the view of her trim backside, curving round and soft beneath her thin pink robe.

Daniel stepped closer, his arms crossed over his chest. "What is so funny?"

"You!" she gasped, then went off into another peal of laughter. "How you can pretend to be so righteous when your mind spends so much time wading through lascivious gutters I'll never understand.''

She wiped tears of mirth from her eyes and laughed some more—at his expense. Confusion hit him. ''I'm not the one who was discussing sexual vagaries on the phone…''

Lace rolled onto her back, yelped and went back to her side, still chuckling. '''Sexual vagaries'? Is that what you thought?''

Her bright green eyes were alight with humor. She looked beautiful and happy and… ''You were discussing domination.''

''Not in bed, you idiot.'' She softened the insult with another chuckle. ''Renee is an older woman who's always allowed her husband to have financial say in their marriage. Now her friends are telling her how he's taking advantage of her, how she should assert herself. It's hogwash, of course, because she doesn't want that responsibility. She's happy letting him handle the major decisions in their lives, and from what she told me, he loves her very much and always puts her best interests first. It's a case of reverse discrimination, and women do it to each other all the time now.''

Daniel felt incredibly stupid. ''What you were saying had nothing to do with sex?''

''You must think my every waking thought, my every action, centers on the physical!''

He shifted. ''Well, yeah.''

That started another round of hilarity that continued to the point where Daniel wanted to strangle her. He sat on the edge of the bed and stared at her in dry annoyance. ''Aren't you overdoing it just a bit?''

She hiccuped and gave him a teasing, watery-eyed

smile. "Oh, but overdoing is evidently what I'm known for. Indulgence. Gluttony, even. Why, I never tire out."

"Lace…"

She rested her head on a pillow and smiled at him. She looked serene, freshened by the laughter. Sweet and innocent. "Why are you so repressed, Daniel?"

"I am not repressed." At least, he didn't think he was. No, certainly not. "Just because I show a modicum of restraint rather than your…*flamboyance,* doesn't mean I'm not a sexual person."

He winced as soon as the words left his mouth. He sounded defensive, and idiotic. And now she'd laugh at him again.

But she didn't. She tipped her head and continued to study him. "Do you think it just might be possible we both have a few misconceptions to iron out?"

"I'll concede the merest possibility could exist."

After a moment she stuck her hand out at him and he took it. "Have I thanked you yet for helping me out today?"

"Not exactly." Her hand felt soft and smooth and small in his own. A woman's hand, offered with integrity. He wrapped his fingers around hers and held her firm.

"Then consider this my show of gratitude. It's the truth, I don't have a lot of family I can rely on. I have no doubt I could have muddled through on my own today, but I'm glad I didn't have to."

The emotion in her gaze unsettled him, touched him to his masculine core. More important than her touch were her words. She'd given him a small piece of herself, trusted him not to turn her words back on her, and he felt ridiculously blessed, as if he'd been given the greatest gift of his life.

He felt so pleased, it scared him.

Daniel released her and stood. "Think nothing of it. But, Lace? You know you can count on Annie as family, and Max."

"And your dad, and Guy?"

He hadn't realized she even knew Guy Donovan, though he should have. Guy was his best friend, practically a brother. He worked at Daniel's father's small local company, fulfilling the spot of oldest son since his dad's rather early retirement, a position Daniel had never aspired to. Guy was close to them all, had even lived with them a good portion of his life, so of course Lace knew him.

With the faintest twinge he had to admit was jealousy, he nodded. "And Dad and Guy."

"And you?" She lowered her gaze, her fingers toying with the lace on a pale blue pillow. "Can I count on you as family?"

He wondered if she deliberately played him. Suspecting she might, he narrowed his eyes and answered more bluntly than he'd intended. "I'm here, aren't I?"

"Hmm." She didn't look as though she believed him, but she kept her thoughts to herself. "I'll get my laundry together tomorrow."

"No, I want you to take it easy tomorrow, too. I'll do it, and no more arguments." He put space between himself and the bed, and while he picked up various pieces of clothing, he felt the warmth of her gaze on him. The last thing he lifted, a sheer red bra that made his vision cloud, unearthed a gilt-framed photo. Daniel studied it a minute and, even before Lace spoke, knew who the woman in the picture must be. The resemblance was very strong.

"That's my mother." Her tone changed, no longer

light with humor or teasing. Now she sounded cautious, distant.

"You look a lot like her."

"My cursed coloring, you mean? She loved it, though for me it's been nothing but a hassle."

Daniel snorted. "You're beautiful and you know it."

"Another compliment? I think I'm losing count." He started to take it back, but she jumped in before he could. "It doesn't matter, Danny, not a bit. What my mother considered her greatest asset has been my biggest handicap. And don't pretend you don't understand. Your attitudes reflect those of the masculine masses. No woman can look like me and be taken seriously."

Lace slid off the bed, her face drawn in real anger, surprising Daniel with the suddenness of it. "Lace…"

"Never mind. I don't even care anymore."

"Then why did you bring it up?" he asked gently, sincerely. She seemed like such an enigma, so hard to fathom, impossible to ignore.

"Because your pain medicine is making me maudlin." She headed for the door, causing him to frown in sympathy over her awkward, faltering gait. "I have calls to make. Try not to eavesdrop this time, okay? I wouldn't want to traumatize your fragile sense of propriety with my blatant sexual discussions."

Daniel watched her limp out, and this time he felt no anger at her disdain, no urge for rebuttal. He felt…sympathy. Something had happened with her mother, something that had possibly helped to mold her into the woman she was today. He wanted to find out what it was, wanted to get to know her better.

He wanted to make love to her until neither one of them could see straight. He just didn't know how to overcome the walls he'd set up between them—but he was now determined to try.

Four

Lace heard a thump in the hallway and went still. She tilted her head to listen, but all she heard was silence. Just as she started to type again, she heard a low curse. Daniel? Had he somehow injured himself while going to the basement to do her laundry? Sometimes the steps were slippery from people trudging in and out through the weather.

Once he'd left the apartment again, she'd washed as thoroughly as she could at the sink and dressed in a loose-fitting caftan of lemon yellow and purple. On her feet she wore thick white socks.

The pain medicine hadn't made her quite so sleepy today, but it did work wonders on relieving her pain. She was even able to sit up in bed, with a soft pillow cushioning her injury, while she worked on Daniel's laptop. She knew she looked ridiculous, but Daniel hadn't said a word. He'd only asked her if she was comfortable.

''Daniel?'' She called his name softly, but received no answer. Slowly sliding out of bed, feeling a smidgeon of worry she didn't want to acknowledge, she went to her bedroom door and peeked out. She could now hear muted shuffling, but couldn't quite pinpoint the sound.

''Daniel?''

''Sorry, Lace. Didn't mean to disturb you.'' He appeared a moment later, his hair sprinkled with snow, his cheeks ruddy from the cold, breathing just a tad too quickly, as if he'd been hurrying.

A sort of truce had fallen between them, like two hostile hostages who decide to work together to make the best of a bad situation. Lace had finally begun to relax, to accept his overwhelming presence filling her home, but now, seeing him again, the thrumming feeling returned and she tingled from head to toe. How did he do it? How did this one particular man affect her so easily—without even trying?

She realized she was staring at him stupidly and blushed. ''You've been outside?''

''I, ah… Shouldn't you be back in bed? It looked like you had a hundred letters to answer.''

''No, only about thirty and I'm almost through.''

''You answer every letter personally?''

''Of course.'' She studied him, and knew in a heartbeat he was up to something. ''All right, give.''

He raised one brow, looking his most autocratic. ''I beg your pardon?''

''Now that would be a sight—you begging.''

He started to speak and she said, ''I want to know what you were doing outside, Daniel. For that matter, I want to know what you're doing in my living room.''

''It's a small room, have you ever noticed that, Lace? Not a lot of space for maneuvering or rearranging.''

"Why in heaven's name would you want to rearrange anything? I have things exactly as I like them."

"Well, as to that…" He hedged a moment longer as Lace leaned against the doorjamb and crossed her arms. He made a sound of disgust. "All right. Ruin the surprise, why don't you? I had to make room for the tree."

"A tree?"

"A small one. A Christmas tree. I bought it when I went out earlier." When she only stared at him, he continued in a defensive tone, "It doesn't seem right for you to not have a tree, Lace. It's Christmas."

She felt the color wash from her face. She pushed around him, but he stayed on her heels, crowding her, and when she came to a staggering halt in the entrance to the living room, he almost bumped into her. She felt his hands settle on her shoulders.

"I haven't had a tree since I was… I can't remember the last time I had a tree."

Quietly, his tone almost a caress, Daniel asked, "Didn't you decorate a tree when you were a little girl?"

She shook her head. "For a long time, my mom was married to this rich guy and he had professional decorators come in and fix a tree that was easily ten feet tall. I was afraid to get near it because I thought I might mess something up and everyone would know. Each bow had been placed just so, you see, and if I moved something, or touched something wrong…"

Daniel squeezed her shoulders again. "We used to decorate our tree with stuff Annie and Max had made. Guy and I would supervise after we'd put on the lights and the star on top. It was funny, because until Max and Annie got big enough, all the ornaments would be around the bottom branches and the top of the tree would be bare. Guy and I would wait until after Annie and Max were in bed, then we'd rearrange things a bit, but we never told them, and they never noticed.'' He hesitated a moment, and she could feel the humor in him, the fond remembrance. ''It was a great tree, full of hodgepodge ornaments.''

She turned to face him. ''Where was your dad?''

Daniel gave a long, weary sigh, his hands falling to his sides and his gaze directed inward. ''After Mom died, Dad couldn't cope with the holidays. He'd give me money and ask me to buy presents for the kids, and I could charge our Christmas dinner at the local market, but he didn't join in with us. He'd stay hidden away, usually up in his room, sometimes he'd even take a vacation away from us, like he does now. I tried to make sure Annie and Max didn't notice that he wasn't there. I tried to sort of fill in, make everything so busy and fun that it wouldn't hurt them.''

Lace wondered who had made sure he wouldn't hurt. No one, evidently. Her throat felt tight and she swallowed. ''I don't have any ornaments or lights or anything.''

''I know. I picked up some stuff.''

He stepped around her and sat on the couch. Out of a large bag, he pulled multicolored twinkle lights and several boxes of ornaments. Almost too many, she thought, for such a small tree. Lace crept forward, afraid to delve into how she felt at that moment. She perched carefully on the seat next to him.

''I did my own tree with white lights, but considering how much you like color, I thought you'd prefer these.''

He took them out of the box and reached to the right of the couch to plug them in. Lace smiled at the rainbow hue of colors. She felt tears but fought them back, busying herself by picking up a box of ornaments. They were small glass balls in gold and silver and red.

''This is better than Christmas morning.'' The words felt inadequate to express her feelings, but the silence was killing her, making it impossible to dredge up conversation. Memories rushed back, painful and filled with longing.

One by one, Daniel pulled things from the bag. A package of red bows. A bright silver star for the top. Several strands of multicolored glass garland. Slippery silver icicles.

Lace choked on a deep breath, then laughed at herself for behaving so foolishly. ''Now I do feel like a queen.''

''I'm glad. Are you up to helping me decorate? Or would you rather just watch?'' He spoke quickly, as if his surprise, his words, embarrassed him, and she wanted to hug him tight, to kiss him all over. ''I wanted to have the tree in the stand before I showed you the other stuff. Just so you couldn't say no. I wasn't sure...''

''I love it. All of it. I'd never say no.''

The words hung in the air, and Lace knew he was thinking of things, other circumstances when he might ask and she might say yes.

Her belly tightened and her breasts ached, as if she needed to wrap her arms around herself—or around him. Daniel bit his upper lip, his gaze glued to hers. He'd shaved when he'd gone home to change clothes, and now she touched his jaw, surprised at how that simple touch made her feel.

''Thank you.''

He continued to watch her, and she knew the exact train of his thoughts, because they were her thoughts, as well. He wanted to kiss her—and she wanted him to. But she knew better. Every day she dealt with the relationships, the broken hearts, that had started with a single kiss.

She searched her mind for a topic to break the sexual tension, but only one unpleasant subject sprang to mind. "My mom hated Christmas almost as much as your dad."

Daniel stepped back. Rather than look disgruntled by her choice to halt the tentative progress of their romantic urges, he seemed intrigued. He knelt by the small tree only partially secured in the stand—a tree no more than four feet in height. As he tightened the bolts that held the trunk, he glanced back at her. "Tell me more about your mother."

Too late to withdraw, Lace prepared herself to divulge personal hurts while watching Daniel tackle the tree. "Mom became something of a pariah in the social standing she aspired to. She married a rich man because he could pamper her, could erase every worry from her brain, and my mother really hated to have to fret over anything. She thought he loved her. I always knew she was only a trophy to him, a much younger woman who looked beautiful and sexy on his arm. I suppose, had he lived, it would have been an even trade. They both got what they wanted.

"But then he died, and everything changed. Mom wanted to go on the same way, to find another man who treated her as gently, who patronized her as richly as he did. But somehow that relationship never transpired. Men saw her in one of two ways, and neither of those ways was overly flattering or involved legitimate caring."

Daniel carried the tree to the corner he'd cleared. Lace stopped him. "You probably know a whole lot more about this tree business than I do, but what would you think of sitting the tree on that small marble-topped table? Wouldn't that make it more noticeable?''

Daniel grinned. ''Of course it would. Do you have an old towel or something we can put underneath so we don't scratch the marble?''

It took a few moments to get the table situated, and already Lace regretted speaking about her mother. The anger she felt on her mother's behalf, and the pity, left a churning pain in her stomach. She didn't want to ruin this special moment, but already her head ached with the memories.

She thought Daniel might have let the subject go. But as soon as he had the tree steady and secure, he brought it up again. ''How did men see your mother, Lace?''

He wasn't fooling her with his casual disregard. She knew his attentive mode and this was it. She'd seen it many times with Annie, when he cared a great deal about the topic, but didn't want to overreact. It didn't matter that he was busy stringing the lights on the tree, or that he hadn't precisely looked at her.

What would happen if she confided in him just a bit? Nothing in the past day and a half seemed real any longer. Certainly not her relationship with Daniel. And if he stopped despising her so much…what then? Maybe her relationship with Annie wouldn't be so strained if Daniel accepted her.

With a bracing breath, she forged onward and hoped for the best. ''My mother found men in two separate classifications. One group wanted to marry her for her money, despite her humble beginnings and the very obvious fact that we'd never fit in, that we weren't in any way part of the rich elite. The other wanted nothing at all to do with her. They turned up their noses and treated her like a tramp, accusing her of marrying for money, of being mercenary enough to be glad her husband was dead.''

''It must have been very difficult for you.''

Lace pondered that. She hadn't often thought about the way it had affected her, she'd been too filled with remorse for her mother. ''She's never stopped trying to find another true love. And I don't have the heart to convince her one doesn't exist.''

Daniel stopped what he was doing. He stared.

''What?'' Lace felt uncomfortable with his scrutiny. ''You're looking at me as if I've grown an extra head.''

He smiled. ''Was I?'' He stood and brushed off his hands, then reached for a box of ornaments. ''Actually, there's two things. You said your mother has never stopped looking for a true love. Do you mean she's still looking?''

Since the placement of the ornaments looked simple enough, Lace picked up a box of her own and went to help. She placed the first one on the tree tentatively, waiting for Daniel to explain that she was doing it wrong. But he didn't say anything, just went about his business, hanging more and more until the tree began to look heavy with color and the ornaments rested in clusters.

''My mother travels every holiday. Actually, she travels almost year round, but especially during the holidays. She says she's lonelier then, and believe me, there's always one man or another more than willing to take advantage of her generosity. After all, it's a free vacation, right?''

Lace knew the sarcasm hung thick in her tone, but she didn't care. Daniel didn't seem to mind. He never once looked at her.

''Mom travels in the best circles, with the ritziest accommodations. She never wants for company, but she always comes back more dejected than ever. I've tried to explain to her that she can't buy love, but she doesn't know any other way. When her husband widowed her, he left her with a group of people she'd come to know, to count on as friends through his association. But they've demolished her self-esteem with their condemnation and criticism. They've ostracized her, and she's still doing her best to find acceptance in the only way she knows how.''

''Was it hard for you, as a young girl, to accept your mother's choices?''

Lace shook her head vehemently, with certainty. But she lied. Of course it hurt. There just wasn't anything she could do about it.

''Lace…''

''Okay, so it used to embarrass me a little. She'd drag me to gatherings with her, happy that she had her daughter and her new man at her side, and we'd all be ridiculed. But then it struck me how unfair I was being. Men do it all the time, exchange lovers like worn shoes. Why shouldn't my mother do the same if that's the lifestyle that suits her?

''People have to deal with their loneliness and heartache in their own way, despite the ramifications involved. Now it only embarrasses me that society is so ridiculous, that a woman is judged harshly by a double standard as outdated as the one that claims she must be pure, while a man is only more appealing with experience.''

''Is that why you condone sexual freedom?''

She rolled her eyes. ''It's why I condone personal choices, made by mature, responsible adults. You make it sound as if I advocate orgies and indiscriminate lechery.''

Daniel considered that, watching her, his eyes thoughtful and his expression intent. After a moment he nodded, but Lace had no idea what conclusions he'd drawn.

''Another thing.'' He draped some garland across a branch, then stood back to admire it. Lace admired it, as well. ''You said you didn't have the heart to convince your mother that true love doesn't exist.''

''It's not my place, even as her daughter, to offer advice when it's not asked for.''

''I understand. But the part that stumped me is your assumption that love isn't real.''

She tried a laugh, but it sounded forced even to her own ears. ''I've seen plenty of relationships begin on the misconception of love, but nothing that could substantiate real love existed. Not the mythical stuff that lasts a lifetime, through thick and thin, sickness and health and all that. All I've seen is an illusion that falls apart easily enough, over the most trivial of things, leaving broken people behind. Lust is real, affection and friendship and common ground. But love…'' She shrugged, feeling helpless with the way he watched her, feeling inadequate to explain what she knew as a truth.

Daniel actually laughed. ''You're wrong, you know. Love is there, and it's all-consuming. I just want no part of it. It does cripple people, when things don't work out. Look at my dad. He loved my mother more than anything.''

And, Lace thought, *even more than his children.* To the point where he couldn't be bothered with them once she'd gone.

''Don't get me wrong. And don't feel pity for me or

my family. Dad's there, and he's as involved as he can be. We all know he cares. It's just that I don't think he'll ever really be able to cope with the loss of my mother. He was always flighty, and she was the one who kept things grounded. They were like two halves, each dependent on the other. Now one half is gone and he isn't whole anymore.''

''And you think that constitutes love as a dangerous thing?'' She thought about it, about his reactions, and nodded to herself. ''It could explain why you're so constrained. You're a product of your environment. I can understand that. Children are often influenced by...''

''Don't be a fool, Lace.'' He thrust his chin toward her, his entire demeanor belligerent.

Familiar ground, she thought.

''I am never foolish, and I only meant—''

''What? To charge me off the clock for a free evaluation? I can't afford you.''

Her face reddened. ''I don't charge people! I'm not a psychologist. I'm a—''

''I know what you are. And believe me, I don't need to be psychoanalyzed.''

She shoved a red bow onto the tree, nearly knocking it over. ''And I don't need you to patronize me. Just because I'm female doesn't mean I don't know my business. I have a master's degree in sex education. I graduated at the top of my class. My radio show is one of the most popular around.'' She tapped a finger against her chest and leaned toward him. ''I'm one of the best in my field, despite my gender or age.''

Daniel caught her hand and curled his own around it. His knuckles brushed her breast and she stilled, going mute in a heartbeat.

With his nose nearly touching hers and his expression

black, he said, "I wasn't trying to discredit your abilities. Believe me, I know the influence you have over others. In Annie's case, you have too much influence." She started to speak, but he laid a quieting finger to her lips. "My turn to talk, okay? Without interruptions."

She nodded since he gave her no other option. The feel of his finger on her mouth, firm and warm, did funny things to her insides.

Slowly, he lowered his hand, allowing it to rest at the side of her neck, causing more reactions to erupt in her belly as he curved his fingers around her throat. His scowl softened and melted away to be replaced by a look of scrutiny. "I've never discriminated against a woman in my life."

She knew that. Time and again she'd seen Daniel show respect and admiration for women and their abilities. He treated all his professional colleagues the same, despite their sex. That attitude, she realized, appealed to her as much as his delectable physical appearance.

His other hand lifted, until he cupped her head between his warm palms. She forgot to breathe, to move away.

"I like touching you, Lace. I'm even finding that I like being around you, when you refrain from dissecting my character, or slicing me to ribbons with your wit."

"You're easy to banter with."

He grinned. "Translated to mean, you can always get the best of me and you like that."

She pursed her lips, modestly holding back her agreement.

"At least we agree on some things. Neither one of us wants anything to do with love. Correct?"

Lace nodded, though she wasn't sure she agreed anymore. She'd told him she didn't entirely believe in love, not that she didn't crave it. At the moment, with him touching her, it seemed like a moot point.

"Will you also agree we've both changed? That this day together has changed us?"

She wanted to agree, but not without verification first. "Explain what you mean."

"I understand you better now, Lace. I know that you're not mindlessly promiscuous, that you're only re-acting to how you've been raised, the examples you've been given by both men and women."

Heat rushed up her spine, making her temples pound, her hands curl into fists.

"Don't misunderstand. I'm not judging your mother, I swear. I'm only attributing her with a due amount of influence on your life. As you just said, children react to the environment they're surrounded in—"

"I think you'd better let me go now."

"Lace?"

"I'm warning you, Daniel." She could barely get the words out through her stiff lips. "You're in serious dan-ger of me laying you low."

He rubbed his hands tiredly over his face, nearly knocking his glasses off, then pressed a fist to his mouth and studied her. He dropped his hands and shrugged. "You're snapping like a wounded pup, and there's really no reason. I'm only trying to be honest with you, Lace."

"Ha!" She wanted to smack him, but held herself in check. Barely. "You're trying to fit me into the little niche you've assigned me. But I have to give you credit, Daniel. You've stepped away from the masculine pack, finding your own unique logic to look down your nose at me. You see, like my mother, I've known two types of men. Those outside the professional field who see me and immediately decide I'm easy, based on my profession and my damned *flamboyant* appearance.''

Daniel winced, probably a mixed reaction to her barely repressed outrage and her use of his description said with such contempt. "I didn't mean…''

She ignored his scowling interruption. "And men *within* my professional circles totally disregard me as a flake. I'm beneath their exalted notice. My credentials, my experience and accomplishments can't possibly matter because I'm a young attractive female and everyone just knows young females aren't to be taken seriously.''

"Lace…''

"But not you, Daniel. Oh, no. You don't want me sexually, because that would make you as real and alive as the rest of us mere mortals, no better than me.'' She felt sick suddenly and groped for the couch, holding on to the padded arm and doing her best to keep her tone level. "At least you don't deny my intelligence or my influence. No, you think I have so much sway, I'm capable of corrupting your poor little innocent sister!''

"Sit down, Lace.''

"Don't you tell me what to do!''

"I am telling you, dammit. You're overreacting and you're ready to collapse.'' Without her permission, he took her arm and lowered her to the cushion. Very quietly, he said, "I didn't mean to upset you, to start another argument.''

"No? What did you mean then? To explain to me why I lack morals so I could look at you, my benevolent instructor, with heartfelt gratitude for straightening it all out for me in my inferior female brain?''

He growled, twisted his fingers in his hair and tugged. Lace watched, bemused and fascinated.

He stared off toward the tree, and Lace looked, too.

The tree looked lovely, though sad. Half finished, without the illumination of the lights, it appeared to be an incomplete project.

The silence dragged out until finally he crouched on the floor beside her. "Look. All I meant was to show you understanding." His gaze captured hers and refused to let her look away.

"Understanding of my sordid way of life? Save it, Doctor."

He took her hand and held it tightly when she tried to yank it away. "I'm sorry. I know how badly I hate it when others try to dissect me—which is exactly what you started to do."

"And you practically snapped my head off!"

"I know. I'm sorry. It stands to reason you wouldn't like it any better than I do. The times when I was younger, when my father more or less abandoned me, though I hate to call it that…they were awful, lonely and scary and uncertain. I think it was probably the same for you. Only you were alone. At least I had Max—trial that he was, and Annie. And Guy was there, helping out."

Lace thought it must have been harder on him because he had people who relied on him. She was free to throw herself into her studies, without outside responsibilities to distract her.

His thumb rubbed over her knuckles and her frown faded away. His mouth tilted in a rueful smile. "I wanted to…comfort you, I suppose. Though that seems ridiculous now because you really are an independent, intelligent woman. I don't suppose you need my comfort."

She needed it now. And she thought he might need a little, as well. With her free hand, she smoothed his hair away from his forehead. "I've enjoyed myself today,

Daniel. Except for the arguing, of course. But it seems we can't be near each other without haggling. Being professional doesn't automatically endow us with a common ground. And it seems like I no sooner see you than my thoughts start toiling on a way to push your buttons.''

One side of his mouth kicked up in a crooked grin. ''You do have a most agile tongue when it comes to putting me in my place.''

''You don't do so badly yourself.''

He hesitated a moment, then forged onward. ''There was something else I wanted to do.''

Her heart began to thump erratically, knocking against her ribs, making her tremble inside and out. She waited for him to lean toward her, to press his mouth against her own. To kiss her...

''I wanted to invite you to my house for Christmas.''

Once again, he'd dumbfounded her. An invitation to spend more time with him was the very last thing she'd anticipated.

''My only excuse for making such a muddle of things is that, well, you confuse my brain, Lace. I think you have since the very first time I saw you.''

Slowly, the smile came, and this time she felt it deep inside herself, making her warm and content. She confused his brain? *That sounded like a good thing.* ''By any chance, is that another compliment?''

He opened his mouth, snapped it shut and frowned. ''The invitation is genuine. Now will you say yes and put me out of my misery, or do I need to remain on my knees all night?''

She shooed him away with her hands. ''Off your knees. Even us queens can only take so much abject devotion.'' When he was standing once again, looking gorgeous and as confused as she felt, one contrary thought after another skittered through her brain. She held her head, then heard herself say, "I'll come for Christmas. If you're sure that's what you want."

In his most officious tone, he said, "Of course I'm certain. I asked, didn't I?"

Lace thought he looked very uncertain, but she held her tongue.

Daniel nodded. "Very good. I'm pleased with your verbal restraint. Now sit back and watch while I put the finishing touches on this tree."

When he plugged in the lights, Lace was so distracted by the beauty of it, the soft glow of a dozen different colors mellowed in the depths of the green tree, she didn't even notice him tack a piece of mistletoe in the arched doorway leading to her kitchen. Not, that is, until he stood beneath it, dogged resolution darkening his features, a crooked finger beckoning her closer.

Five

Every muscle in his body pulled tight, including the most vital ones, when Lace slowly, deliberately, came to her feet. He wanted to tease, to claim kissing under mistletoe as a family tradition, which it was, but he was afraid if he tried to speak, he'd only groan. Or maybe confess how much he craved her.

She came nearer and nearer in her injured, halting step, still so feminine, so sweetly sensual with her every movement. She made him want to hold her close, to swear to her nothing would ever hurt her again. He held still until she stood only an inch or two from touching him. Common sense warred with basic need. Need won.

His fingers lifted to her hair. It felt so soft, like Lace herself, and looked so pale he'd often wondered if the shade was real. Finding out would be more fun than his poor afflicted heart could endure. It was also an event greatly anticipated.

He no sooner thought it than he pulled back. His heart wasn't involved, not in any way, only his groin, only his masculine genes and his libido—which raged with encouragement. He wanted her, a simple, straightforward physical reaction, a circumstance suffered by all men.

Only there was nothing straightforward or simple about Lace McGee, or his reaction to her.

As an adult—a *responsible mature adult*—there would be nothing wrong in the two of them deciding on a brief affair. Or rather, a long, hot, gritty affair. Getting Lace out of his system wasn't going to happen overnight. And he wanted her out. Didn't he?

Lace stared up at him, one slim eyebrow cocked. "Are you going to kiss me or not?"

So much impatience. He smiled. "I believe I am." Her mouth looked rosy and ready and anxious. He tightened his thighs and braced himself to keep from throwing her on the couch and showing her just how badly he wanted to kiss her, to eat her alive.

She smirked. "I don't mean to rush you through whatever masculine ruminations you're presently pursuing, Daniel, but I do wish you'd hurry up with it. The suspense is about to kill me."

He laughed, despite the gravity of the situation, despite his now painful arousal. "You have such a way with words."

"You hate my way with words."

He shrugged. "You're starting to grow on me."

"Moss could grow on you, you move so slowly."

Chuckling, he asked, "Is that a hint?"

She heaved a huge sigh, and his gaze was drawn to her breasts, loose beneath her clothing. He forced his gaze more northerly, to avoid a loss of control.

"It's a statement, telling you I'm about to get bored and walk away."

"We can't let that happen." He leaned down, watching her go still and breathless, and he brushed his mouth over hers, teasing himself, barely tasting her when he wanted to taste her so badly. He wanted his tongue in her mouth, their teeth clashing, her body pressed flush against his so he could grind his hardening flesh into her soft belly. He shuddered with the thought and subsequent reaction of his body.

Such a dangerous game, one that could trip him up and leave him flat on his face. For months now he'd been vehemently trying to prove, both to himself and to her, that he didn't want her. He'd played at being immune when in truth she affected every pore in his body. Even his teeth and toenails ached in need whenever Lace entered the same room as him. Lately, whenever he even thought of her.

But all mankind knew the power of male pride. How could he claim to just change his mind, to give in, without making it look as though he'd been wrong all along? How could he claim to want her sexually without losing his male consequence? He stared down at Lace, pondering the problem.

"Is that it? Is that the best you could do?"

Daniel laughed, but quickly sobered. She was serious. She hadn't even realized the deliberation of his kiss, the temptation of moving slowly, the finesse involved in teasing so delicately. His awesome style was totally wasted on her. Well, hell. Her brow puckered and her eyes were alert, if a bit disappointed.

Just that quickly, a plan took root, an ingenious way for him to salvage his ego and still have her. He tried to wipe the elation off his face and strove for a look of consternation. "You didn't like it?"

She gave a rude snort. "I got kissed better than that when I was in first grade."

"Started young, did you?"

She opened her mouth and he said, "Forget I asked." Once again, he brushed his mouth against hers, this time making all efforts at a lackluster effect, doing his best to restrain the fierce urge to devour her with his mouth and tongue. "Better?"

"Uh, no. Not really."

He had to bite his lip to keep from chuckling. "You're not one much for false flattery, are you?" Before she could answer, he plastered his mouth to hers, keeping his lips closed, barely moving, but damn, she felt good, tasted good, smelled good. He wanted to devour her, to thrust his tongue deep and feel her breasts against his chest, to hear her choppy breathing. To kiss her mouth, her throat, her breasts and her belly.

His heartbeat thundered, reverberating through his body to collect in a single pounding pulse in his groin. He forced himself to pull away before he lost his meager control. Ridiculously, his hands shook.

"Daniel," she moaned, and her arms went around his neck. For the briefest instant he forgot his new game and held her close, his mouth opening on hers, his tongue touching her bottom lip, the edge of her teeth. She groaned again and he wanted, in that instant, to have her naked, warm and willing, beneath him. He wanted her eager and involved. He wanted to experience firsthand everything she knew and condoned about sexual freedom, and he wanted her to beg him to show her what he knew.

But she was injured and any involved intimacy would

have to be put off anyway, so there was really no reason for ruining his plan.

"Do you like your tree?" He spoke in a hushed, husky whisper. Getting the words formed in his muddled brain took nearly all his concentration.

"I love my tree." She tried to find his mouth again, but he turned his face toward her neck, nuzzling the soft skin there, breathing gently in her ear.

He felt her trembling increase. *"Daniel."*

"Time for lunch." He made the announcement at the same time he eased away from her. Damn she was good. But then, he'd already known that.

He didn't want to hurt her, her wounded body or her delicate emotions, so he had to move with care.

"Lunch?"

He couldn't look at her or all would be lost. He held his control by only a snippet of a thread. "You need to eat while taking the pain medication and the antibiotics, and with all you've been through, you need to keep up your strength."

She searched his face and her breath still came too fast. "Of course. Food. I was just about to suggest the very same thing."

He kept a straight face with much effort. "I'm going to run down and check on the laundry, then I'll warm everything up. Why don't you finish your correspondence?"

"I only have a few more letters to see to." So saying, she slipped on down the hall, her entire countenance dejected.

Daniel could finally grin. He had her now. She cared about the people she helped, that much was plain. He'd watched her frown her way through tough decisions, ponder for long moments her every reply. She took her work as seriously as he took his own.

He rubbed his hands together, anxious to become one of her cases. She already thought him repressed, and heaven knew how chaotic and busy his life had always been, between med school and tending his brother and sister. It wasn't beyond the realm of possibility that he might be sexually inept. Highly unlikely, but not impossible. So he was thirty-five? Age meant nothing. It certainly wasn't proof that he'd have a wealth of experience at his disposal. And his ego wasn't so tender that he couldn't *pretend* to need help in order to gain Lace's trust.

He'd always been very discreet, not wanting to set a bad example for Annie. Plus, he'd needed to counteract Max's lack of discretion. His younger brother seemed to sow more than his fair quota of wild oats. And with his travels, he'd probably sowed oats in more fields all over the country than any three men put together.

No, Lace would find no evidence of his expertise. He'd let her lead him, gently, into intimacy. He'd give her complete control over his body. The mere thought was enough to make him howl with lust.

He was still considering all the finer points of his plan when he hurried back to the door of Lace's apartment. The laundry basket in his arms all but blocked his vision, and suddenly he bumped into a body coming out of the stairwell.

"Excuse me." He lowered the basket, took in the stunned, familiar face peering up at him, then immediately tried to raise the basket again.

Annie didn't let him get away with it. She snatched the basket out of his hands and dropped it on the floor between them. A pair of turquoise panties tumbled out onto the floor, landing on top of Daniel's shoe. They both stared at them a moment, until Daniel snatched them up and put them back on top of the basket. His sister gaped.

"Dan!" Annie looked from him to the basket and back again. "What in heaven's name are you doing here?"

With a wry grimace and an inward curse at fate, he waved at the basket. "Laundry."

Lace wondered what was keeping Daniel.

Then she wondered at that kiss. Not that she was any expert on the actuality of the subject, but something hadn't seemed quite right. With the way she'd always felt around him, she'd been expecting to be swept off her feet. And in one regard she had. She'd loved the feel of his mouth, the drift of his breath on her cheek, the warmth of his large, strong body so close to her own. Warm, tingly feelings had stirred in her lower belly and her nipples had felt tight, too sensitive. Strangely enough, she'd wanted him to touch them, to touch her.

But he'd seemed…tentative. Unsure. She'd always known Daniel had a hang-up where she was concerned, but she'd never considered his attitude might stem from inexperience. Now she had to reevaluate.

He was simply too gorgeous, too worldly, too… sought after. Somehow she couldn't imagine a woman looking at him and not wanting him. And somehow she hadn't thought he'd always refuse.

Well, no one had said he was entirely without experience, but surely, even a *little* experience would have taught the man how to kiss. And rigid? He'd held himself like a pike, not moving, barely breathing. He sure wasn't the romancer she'd expected him to be. She felt terrible for teasing him for so long, potentially compounding his problem with sex.

In one regard, she was glad he lacked hands-on confidence. At least it meant he wasn't a hypocrite.

In another way, the thought of him being inexperienced made her giddy with excitement. She wondered how he would react if she set out to educate him. She thought she could probably manage it with a little luck and a lot of forethought. And assisting him could be just the excuse she needed to appease her overwhelming desire.

Having Daniel in her home had changed everything, had shown a different side of him, a more human, considerate, understanding side. She could no longer fight her own natural desires. But she didn't want to look as if all the antagonism between them hadn't mattered, and she simply couldn't concede the contest of wills, not when he'd made such erroneous assumptions about her character.

When she heard a noise at the door, she decided to test him just a bit with a taste of verbal innuendo. She lowered her voice to what she hoped was a sultry, sexy tone, then called out, ''Daniel? Is that you, finally? It's really unfair of you to stir up my appetite and then leave me waiting.'' She giggled at her own ridiculous verbiage before adding, ''I'm starved!''

She wondered if he'd assume she meant the food he promised, or if he'd detect the sexual undertones of her words. She heard approaching footsteps and laid her head against the pillows in what she hoped represented an inviting pose. Much of the pain had eased and she could once again use her backside for the purpose intended—sitting. But she had to be cautious and the seat needed to be soft. Unfortunately, she didn't think Daniel's lap would qualify.

With her head tilted just so and a winsome smile on her mouth, she waited until he came through the doorway, then murmured, ''It's about…time…''

''Ha!'' Annie laughed out loud, her blue eyes dancing. A thick braid held her long dark hair, which hung down her back, swishing near her trim hips. Her parka was unzipped to show a close-fitting red sweater and dark jeans. As always, she looked pretty and vibrant and happy. Daniel had done a good job with her, Lace thought.

Lace jerked upright, only to have Annie rush around the bed and shove her back again. ''No, don't you dare get up on my account. Daniel told me what happened. How awful for you!'' She glanced at Lace's bottom half, then asked in a whisper, ''Does it hurt?''

''Not any more—''

''I'm so sorry I wasn't home when you needed me! Especially after all the help you've given me.'' She embraced Lace, and over Annie's shoulder, Lace saw Daniel step into the room and set the filled laundry basket on the floor. He stood in the doorway, took in his sister's effusive regret and rolled his eyes.

Lace pulled herself together. ''Annie, really, I'm fine.''

''No, no, you're not. Daniel told me *everything*.''

Uh-oh. ''Daniel has already explained?''

''Yes, and now this proves what a sweetie he is. Didn't I tell you he was just the most *wonderful* brother? Maybe now you'll believe me.''

Daniel cleared his throat. He didn't look particularly sweet at the moment. He look disgruntled—and back to his former aloof self. "I'll let Annie put your things away while I get the food heated up."

Because it hurt to see the distance back in his expression, Lace turned to Annie. "Will you stay and eat with us?"

"I suppose, if there's enough. What are you having?"

"Mexican. Hot." Then she turned to Daniel, her look pointed. "What exactly do we have to eat?"

"A little of everything. Fajitas, tacos, burritos, nachos. Lots of salsa and cheeses. And lots of jalapeños and red chilies."

Annie's eyes widened. "Yum! I'd love to join you."

Lace slanted Daniel a look of smug satisfaction, determined to goad him out of his mood. "Your little sister likes *spicy* food as much as I do."

Annie agreed. "I love it, now that Lace has gotten me hooked on it."

To Lace's disappointment, Daniel left the room without a single comment.

"So, tell me. What's really going on?" Without reserve, Annie began opening drawers and closets, shoving clothing inside. Annie was not exactly the epitome of domesticity. Household chores often escaped her realm of understanding.

Lace cleared her throat and took her time gathering up her correspondence. "I don't know what you mean. What did Daniel tell you was going on?"

"He said you got hurt, there was no one else to take care of you, so he stepped in. He said he knew I'd have his head if he left you here alone, and he was right."

Lace frowned. So he didn't want Annie to know he'd kissed her. Probably because he didn't want to corrupt her poor little impressionable mind by letting her think he'd cavort with a woman of Lace's ilk. The big jerk.

Annie patted her hand. "I know there's more to it than that, though."

"Oh? How so?" Lace hoped she looked suitably confused.

"I offered to stay with you, to let him go home now, but he refused. He said I wasn't qualified to take care of you." She snorted. "I can toady for a person as easily as he can."

Lace winced as Annie crammed her T-shirts into a drawer. "Daniel isn't *toadying* for me."

"He's doing your laundry, for crying out loud! What would you call it? And that tree. I saw it the minute I came in and thought you'd finally softened and gotten one. But when I commented on it, he told me he'd done it. He mumbled it, like it embarrassed him or something. Wasn't that sweet of him, Lace?"

The sisterly admiration on Annie's face wasn't to be refuted. "He's been very kind. At select and individual moments."

Daniel called them in to eat, and Annie helped Lace out of the bed, even though she didn't need help. Once they were in the kitchen, Lace felt stymied. There was no way she could sit in one of the hard-bottomed chairs. Daniel touched her shoulder.

"Hold on just a second. I'll be right back."

He went down the hall to her bedroom and returned a moment later with a fat bed pillow. He placed it on the chair, then took her arm. "See how that feels."

Annie watched on as if fascinated while her brother solicitously seated Lace. Once she'd lowered her bottom onto the soft pillow, he pulled another chair forward for her to prop her legs on.

"Keep your leg elevated. It'll help to keep the pressure off the wound."

Then he served her a plate.

Lace felt like an inconsiderate witch, especially with the pleased admiration shining on Annie's face. Daniel had waited on her all day, made certain she'd taken her antibiotics and her pain pills on schedule. He'd fed her and teased her and given her a tree. He'd even washed her dirty laundry, which went well beyond the realm of consideration. She wanted to cry. She should have been more grateful, not resentful that he wanted to keep the kiss between them private.

When she took her first bite of chili, she nearly did cry. Her mouth caught on fire and she fanned her hand in front of her open mouth. Daniel handed her a glass of water, and she knew if she looked at him, he'd be wearing a smug expression. Spicy indeed!

She'd told him she liked her Mexican food hot. Well, it couldn't get much hotter than this.

"Wow!" Annie was the next to suffer from the jalapeño peppers liberally mixed into everything. She grabbed for her own glass of water, sputtering and choking.

Daniel looked at them both with teasing contempt. "Tenderfoots." He wolfed down his own food with a distinct show of relish for their amazement.

Both Annie and Lace laughed at his uncharacteristic display. Lace saluted him, then doused her own food with plenty of salsa and cheese to mellow it enough to be edible. Altogether, it was so delicious, and she ate so much, she knew she wouldn't be hungry the rest of the day.

The meal lingered, mixed with conversation and laughter, for more than two hours. Lace watched Daniel and Annie interact. The way he smiled at his sister, with unconditional love and acceptance, amused by her every word, made Lace ache inside. She couldn't begin to fathom the depth of their dedication to each other.

"I bought you the perfect gift, Lace. You're going to love it."

Lace froze with her fork in midair and her mouth open. "You bought me a present? Why?"

Annie laughed at her in amazement. "It's almost Christmas, silly." She winked at Daniel. "I love buying gifts almost as much as I like getting them."

Daniel shook his head. "I haven't even starting shopping yet, Annie, so stop giving me that look. You'll have to wait until Christmas morning and be surprised like the rest of us."

Lace listened to them with half an ear. It made her uncomfortable to know she was now honor bound to do her own Christmas shopping. She hadn't purchased holiday gifts for anyone in too many years to count. For the most part, she'd always ignored the holidays. Now she wouldn't be able to. She wasn't at all certain if that was a good or a bad thing.

"I have a few more errands to run, but I'll come back and spend the night with you."

Before Lace could find the right words to refuse Annie's offer, Daniel spoke up. "She needs her sleep tonight, Annie, and I know how women are. You two would sit up all night gabbing."

Lace could have debated how well he knew women, given the demonstration she'd had so far, but she truly did want some time alone.

"Really, Annie, I'm fine now. I won't be hopscotching anytime soon, but I can manage."

"You're sure? What if you need something?"

"If she needs you, she can call. Her phone is right by her bed."

Annie stared at Daniel, and he shrugged. "I'll make certain she's settled before I leave this evening, Annie. There's no need for you to worry."

Lace felt all too conspicuous with them speaking about her. She interjected in what she hoped was an aggrieved tone. "All I really need is a hot shower to work out some of the stiffness from sitting around all day, but I think that's out of the question."

Daniel retrieved Annie's coat for her. As she slipped it on, taking the not-so-subtle hint with good grace, Daniel turned to Lace.

"If you really want a shower, I can arrange it."

"A magician, are you? I specifically heard the nurse tell me not to get the stitches wet for a while."

They both walked Annie to the door. "You could use an aqua-guard, a plastic adhesive patch you put over the stitches to keep them dry. I wouldn't want you to soak in a tub, but a quick shower should be okay if you apply the patch correctly."

Annie smiled and mouthed the word, *Wonderful,* behind Daniel's back, then gave them both a hug goodbye. "Promise you'll call me if you need anything, Lace."

"I promise, but I'll be fine."

"I trust you to take good care of her, Dan."

"I intend to."

Once the door closed behind her, Lace felt self-conscious. The memory of their kiss hung in the air between them. Daniel hesitated a mere second, then pulled her close, gently curling her into his body until she felt surrounded by his heat and his strength and she realized how much she'd missed it since the last time he'd held her. She'd grown addicted to his touch in such a very short time.

She tipped up her face and he kissed her again.

This kiss was a little less awkward, but still very brief. He touched his mouth to the bridge of her nose, her forehead; his cheek rubbed hers as he ran his fingers through her hair, over her skull, cupping her gently. She felt lulled, enticed.

Lace moved back enough that she could see his face, the tenderness in his expression. It moved her so much, she closed her eyes to guard against it and parted her lips, silently asking to have his mouth instead. He nipped her bottom lip, surprising her and making her eyes snap open again.

"The aqua-guard might be a little difficult for you to put on yourself."

His tone was gentle, low. Lace tried to reconcile his words with the mood she presently floated in. "Aqua-guard?"

"The plastic patch I told you about. So you could shower. Given where the dog bit you, it might be difficult for you to get it on properly."

Lace jerked back. "You're not suggesting I let you help me with it?"

He stared at her mouth. "Why not? I'm your doctor. I'll have to check it again tomorrow sometime anyway. And when the stitches are ready to come out."

"Not on your life." Lace had no intention of returning as a patient to the hospital, or of baring her injury to Daniel's interested eyes.

Daniel chucked her chin. "Don't look so appalled. If you think you can manage, that's fine. But do it now while I pick up the mess in the kitchen so if you do have a problem, you can let me know."

"As if I would," she muttered. Lace turned away, horrified by the mere thought. Daniel stopped her with a hand on her arm.

"Come with me to the kitchen. When I got your prescriptions filled, I picked up a couple of the patches just in case."

Lace trailed behind him, feeling the heat in her cheeks. She imagined the ignonimous position she'd have to be in to apply the patch, and knew he could easily imagine the same. She covered her face with one hand.

"I'm a doctor, Lace. You have no reason to be embarrassed."

"That little truism helps not one iota."

It wasn't easy, but she did manage to get the patch in place. As she quickly showered, she wondered just how long he intended to hang around. He couldn't spend the night again because he had to be at the hospital very early the next day. She needed him to go so she could sort out her feelings and the strange, seductive plan she'd almost reconciled herself to.

Could she actually give Daniel Sawyers, the epitome of sobriety and discretion, lessons on sexual expression?

She'd never know until she tried. And there was never a better time than the present.

Daniel paced, wondering how exactly to initiate his newest strategy on Lace. He supposed he could just fumble around enough that she'd take pity on his inept methods and insist on taking the lead. But somehow it seemed better to come right out with it, to get her agreement up front.

He went through her CD collection as he listened to the water running and imagined Lace naked in the shower, her slim body wet and white and so very soft. He groaned. Damn, but she made him nearly crazy. His errant thoughts skipped ahead, erotic images forming in his mind of her naked, sitting astride his hips, giving him direction.

He'd gladly do anything she asked.

But first he had to get her to do the asking. How to do it?

He put on a country classic Christmas collection he'd brought in earlier from his car and while he listened to the music, he let his mind wander. He jumped a good foot when Lace suddenly touched his shoulder.

Whipping around, he sucked in his breath and every plan in his tormented mind fled, replaced by raw need. She looked beautiful, damp and warm and rosy cheeked. Her wet hair had been combed straight back from her forehead, emphasizing her high cheekbones and her narrow nose, the bright green of her wide eyes.

She'd changed clothes again. It seemed to him she switched outfits often, and every colorful ensemble she put on made his wits numb and his body hungry. This time she wore a long, straight mauve gown with fitted sleeves and a scooped neckline. A hostess gown, he thought it might be called, though where that errant thought had come from he couldn't imagine. She stood there staring at him, looking more enticing by the second, and he couldn't wait a moment more.

He pulled her close and kissed her. At the last second he remembered to botch it, and he let their noses bump, let his glasses get in the way.

Lace huffed in frustration. She shoved him back a few inches and looked him in the eye. "Are you deliberately trying to make me crazy or what?"

Blushing on cue would have been impossible, but he felt his neck turn red, which he supposed could only assist his efforts.

Trying to look downcast, he said, "I'm sorry. I know I'm not very good at this."

"This?"

He gestured at her, down her body and back up again. Then because he couldn't help himself, he kept on looking until Lace cleared her throat, demanding his attention. "Responding with a sexy woman," he blurted. "I suppose you expected better of me?"

He peeked at her and saw her frown. Excellent.

Then she sighed again. "Not really."

He faltered, forgetting his act and giving her a double take. "No?"

"So far, everything about you has indicated you're not very at ease in sexual situations."

He didn't quite know how to respond to that. A show of masculine outrage would be out of place, given his plan. A demonstration of his sexual ease would ruin everything.

His hesitation prompted her to words. "It's all right, Daniel. I understand."

Humph. She didn't understand anything, least of all him or his sexuality. He cleared his throat. "Most women don't. It's the truth, Lace, my love life is in terrible shape."

He could feel her concern, her caring, and he almost felt like a cur for misleading her. But determination and blind need overruled his finer sensitivities and he stuck with his plan.

Her small hand touched his shoulder, and just that, a simple touch in the most innocuous of places, made his pulse thrum.

"Daniel?" When he didn't answer, she said in the gentlest tone he'd ever heard from Lace McGee, "Look at me."

He did.

"There's nothing to be embarrassed about."

"Ha! It's not every day a man has to admit he's no good as a lover."

Her eyes widened and he wondered if perhaps he was laying it on a bit thick. Not many men would ever admit to such a thing. The realization came too late.

Lace's expression softened, and she smiled at him. "What makes you think you're no good?"

"Hoards of disgruntled women?" He hadn't expected her to doubt him, only to help him.

She laughed. "Hoards, huh? Well, I'll let you in on a secret. This is the time of liberation. A woman is responsible for her own pleasure."

She spoke without embarrassment, much the way he'd been told she spoke on the radio. Lace discussed everything imaginable, to hear others tell it, and never once showed a hint of inhibition. Suddenly the thought inflamed him.

She stroked his shoulder. "If a woman is dissatisfied, it's up to her to tell her lover why, to instruct him, to guide him. Men aren't mind readers. And every woman is different."

Fascinated, he asked, "How so?" just to hear her keep talking. Listening to Lace orate on sexual issues was like extended foreplay; he felt stroked by her voice. How he'd ever last until she was recovered from her wounds was going to be his greatest hardship. He wanted her to start her instructions now. He'd gladly sacrifice his body for the lesson.

"Women all respond to different things, different games, touches, intensity. Some women like subtlety, others blatant advances. Tenderness can be a big turn-on, or rough play, or raw sexuality or…"

Daniel groaned. He'd tortured himself enough for one day. He reached for her—and was interrupted, or perhaps saved, depending on how you looked at it, by a rather loud knocking on the door.

Even as he cursed the fates and silver-tongued women bent on seduction, Lace went to answer her door.

Six

Lace pulled her door open and Max Sawyers whisked in. "Hello, sweetheart."

Lace started in surprise, then gasped when Max jerked her close in his brawny arms and bobbed his eyebrows. "You're under the mistletoe," he said, and Lace looked up, seeing the most ridiculous hat perched on Max's handsome head, a long wire suspending a sprig of mistletoe away from the hat to loom above her.

"Good grief, Max, wherever did you get that thing?"

"Good favor shone on me last night while I was shopping, buying your Christmas present. I saw this hat and knew it was just the thing to get you where I wanted you."

"And where's that?"

He grinned, a roguish tilting of his sensual mouth that probably made female hearts flutter with great anticipation. But Lace was immune, a fact that continued to nettle Max and prod him onward in his amorous pursuit.

He leaned close, still grinning, and whispered, ''Right here, in my arms. Ready to be kissed.''

Lace flattened her palms against his chest and stiffened her arms, putting as much space between them as she could, even as she laughed. He whirled her around, lifting her off the floor so her feet swung in the air behind her and she lost her balance. She landed hard against his solid chest. Her gasp of pain sounded just as Daniel unglued himself from the living room floor and stormed up to his brother.

''Dammit, Max, knock it off!'' He grabbed his brother and pulled him away from Lace, then put his arm around her waist to support her. She sagged against him, relieved to have his rescue. To Lace, he asked, ''Are you all right? You're as pale as a ghost.''

Lace managed a nod, though in truth Max's actions had sent pain singing up and down her thigh and bottom. She could barely stand on her injured leg.

Max stepped closer, his brows pulling down. ''What's going on? What's wrong with Lace?''

''She's injured, you idiot.''

''Well, how was I to know?''

Lace held up a hand. ''Please, it's no big deal.'' Briefly she explained the dog bite to Max and he whistled, twisting around and trying to get a look at her bottom. Daniel scowled, physically manuevering her so that Max couldn't see a single thing.

''Damn, that's horrible. I'm sorry, babe.''

Daniel's arm stiffened around her and Lace pulled away to prop herself delicately on the edge of the couch. She watched the two brothers, aware of the outrage about to erupt and helpless to defuse it.

"What the hell did you think you were doing, busting in here and attacking her?"

Max lifted his brows, eyeing his brother curiously. "I didn't attack her. Well, not really. And I was only trying to steal a kiss, like I always do."

Any minute now, Lace expected to see lightning to match the thundercloud of Daniel's expression. He transferred his glare from Max to her. "Do you have something going on with my little brother?"

"Of course I do." When Daniel blanched, she added, "It's called friendship, you idiot."

His mouth fell open; seconds later he snapped it shut and a red flush ran up his neck. "I'm sorry."

"Sure you are. Sorry that I'm not proving to be the stereotypical nympho you've envisioned?"

Max looked on with interest. "You want Lace to be a nympho? Come to think of it, that's not a bad—"

They both snapped "Shut up, Max!" at the same time. Max held up his hands in a placating gesture, and his mouth twitched as he fought a smile.

"I can't believe you honestly thought I'd sleep with your little brother."

Max stifled a chuckle, then stepped backed when they both glared at him.

Pointing a finger at her, Daniel turned back to Lace. "I never said—"

"You thought it! And what about Guy? Is he safe from my evil, lascivious clutches? As far as that goes, is any male safe? I mean, it's obvious I have no sense of discrimination, no standards to uphold, no—"

Daniel loomed over her. "That's enough, Lace."

"Why? You don't like having your own nauseating misconceptions thrown in your face?"

Max cleared his throat loudly, interrupting the sudden

silence in the room. "Hey, I've never been in here before. Nice place, Lace."

Somehow she couldn't quite force her gaze away from Daniel's. They stared at each other, and it was like touching, a physical, tactile thing that left her energized. "I'm glad someone likes it."

Daniel growled. "I like it, all right? How many times do I need to say it? I like your damned apartment."

Lace crossed her arms over her chest and looked away. Max started backing toward the door. "Look, I think it's time for me to leave. All this hostility is bad for a man of my young impressionable years. Lace, I hope you're feeling better soon." He saluted his brother. "Dan, I hope you shut up before she kills you." Then he laughed and hurried out the door.

Lace could feel herself heaving, her breath coming too fast, her turbulent emotions boiling near the surface. She felt…vital, alive and invigorated. The way she always felt when she sparred with Daniel.

She'd never before realized how easily she spoke with him, how comfortable she was saying anything at all to him. She held no reserve with him, no boundaries. Even his insults no longer seemed so important, now that she thought she understood him. And as she thought of it, she considered the possibility that he might have been a little jealous of Max. Heaven knew, he could take lessons from his little brother when it came to seduction.

"I'm not going away, Lace, no matter how hard you wish it."

She turned to him. "I don't wish any such thing."

"No?"

She shook her head. "Would it really bother you so badly if I got involved with Max?"

Instead of answering, he went perfectly still and asked, "Are you considering it?"

"No, never."

He immediately relaxed. "Why?"

"Because he doesn't know what he wants. He's unsettled. Max is not who you think he is."

Daniel stepped closer, encouraged by her casual tone and lack of vehemence. "No? Then who is he?"

"I don't know yet, mostly because he doesn't know. I think he's confused by his role in the family. He's not the oldest son, the responsible one. And he certainly can't compete with Annie as the youngest and the only female. Guy has become your best friend, taking over your place in the family company. I think Max is still trying to figure out where he fits in."

"Max is my brother, my only brother. He doesn't need to *fit in.*"

"Of course he does. He's twenty-seven years old and he needs his own position in the family. Something with more stature than the overachiever's brother."

Daniel didn't deny being an overachiever, but he did frown.

Lace felt encouraged. "That's why he's always so outrageous. Because he doesn't yet know what to with himself, and being outrageous is a way of covering that up."

"Lace?"

She stared up at him.

He lifted a hand to her cheek. "I don't want to talk about Max anymore."

"What do you want to talk about?" Her skin felt too warm, as if added heat pulsed just beneath. A sweet, tingling sensation swirled low in her belly, pulling tighter with every second that Daniel watched her. Every place his gaze touched on her, she felt it.

"I want to kiss you again. Hell, I want to make love to you and hear you groan." He cupped her face and his hands trembled. "I want you to whisper my name and scream in pleasure."

Lace sucked in a breath. Daniel's brown eyes had softened to a golden glow behind his glasses. She licked her lips and heard him make a small sound of pleasure.

"I...I think I want that, too."

He shook his head. "I don't want to screw up with you."

She knew what he meant, and his sexual insecurity removed her own. "I'll help."

His nostrils flared and his thick lashes swept down to shield his eyes. "Do you understand what I'm saying, Lace? I don't want to fumble things. I want this to be good for you."

"Daniel." She touched his jaw, the side of his throat, and reveled in the warmth of his flesh. "I know you're uncertain. But it'll be okay. I promise."

"You don't mind...instructing me?"

His voice dropped, low and husky and aroused, and Lace wondered at his reaction. Was he really so nervous at the prospect of making love to her? Her heart softened.

No! Not her heart. She would not get emotionally involved with Daniel Sawyers. Their worlds were too different for them to ever harmonize for any length of time. She would not be drawn in by him, by his vulnerability and need. He was just a man, as flawed as any man. As a therapist, she could help him, and take her own pleasure in the bargain, but she wouldn't let him confuse the issues.

"Daniel, do you think you can accept a brief affair with me?"

He stiffened, and Lace thought he might balk. He hesitated, the intensity of his gaze boring into hers. After a long, nerve-stretching moment, he leaned down and kissed her. Another brief, unsatisfying kiss. But she intended to change all that very soon.

"I don't want an involvement any more than you do, Lace."

She swallowed her hurt, insisting to herself that it was exactly the reply she'd wanted. "Good. Then we're agreed."

Daniel touched the tip of her nose. "There's just one thing. As your doctor, I insist you wait awhile before embarking on any amorous adventures. No, don't frown at me. I know what I'm saying. You need to let yourself heal, Lace, to let the stitches do their work."

"And until then? Do we just go on as usual, baiting and sniping at each other?"

"No. I'm not sure I could, in any case. You'll take it easy, I'll check on you occasionally, and you'll come to my house for Christmas. It'll give us both a chance to get used to the idea of being together."

Lace didn't need to get used to the idea, but she supposed Daniel might. This was all new to him. Not that she was the experienced expert he thought. She'd no more hopped in and out of beds than a tadpole hopped from lily pad to lily pad. But that was her own business, not Daniel's. And in the way of understanding sexual drives and urges, she certainly was the expert.

She stuck out her hand and waited for him to take it. "So, we have a deal?"

Daniel shook her hand. "Deal."

Lace wrapped her arms around his neck and pulled

his mouth down to her own. "I think we should seal this particular bargain with a kiss." This time she didn't give Daniel the chance to pull away. She took her time and exploited every trick she knew to make him crazy with need.

When she finally released him, his glasses were fogged and his face was dark with lust.

"You're an evil woman, Lace."

She accepted the insult with a grin, then patted his cheek. "Don't worry, Danny. When the time comes, I'll be gentle with you."

His eyes flashed, and he said in a whisper, "I can hardly wait."

Lace was seriously considering writing a book on extended verbal foreplay. Her experiences with Daniel would serve as the perfect data.

It had been a week since the conception of their plan, and Daniel had utilized his time well. He'd managed to insinuate himself so deeply into her thoughts, not a moment passed that he didn't in some way interrupt her work or her routine. She'd find herself smiling for the most absurd reasons, but try as she might, she couldn't banish him from her brain.

She remembered when he'd stopped by to check up on her because she'd refused to let him remove her stitches. He'd complained endlessly about her defection to another physician. That same day, she'd found him looking through her collection of books. Not fiction for entertainment, but what she considered her texts, books on sexuality, on various other cultures and condoned behaviors.

She'd thought to tease him. "Find one with a lot of pictures, did you?"

He'd looked down at her, his eyes warm with desire, and shown her the book. "Yes, this picture." She'd blushed at the intriguing position of the couple and felt Daniel's gaze on her, watchful. "I'd like to try this with you, Lace."

She shook, just imagining such a thing. And then he'd whispered, "I bet you taste so damn good…"

Lace had refrained from teasing him further.

Now she was tired, having worn herself out with her first full day out of the apartment. Daniel had gotten the day off work and chauffeured her around, and she hadn't bothered to deny him. She liked being with him too much, and she still wasn't comfortable enough to drive herself.

"You look exhausted. Let's call it quits."

"Not yet. One more stop, okay?" They'd been to the radio studio, where she'd checked to make certain everything was ready for her next show. She presented her producer with the letters she'd share on the air and the topic she wanted to cover, and they went over the format. Daniel had watched, looking uncomfortable.

Next they'd had lunch in the mall and Lace had managed to get some of her Christmas shopping done with Daniel's help. She found it wasn't nearly the chore she'd anticipated, in fact, it was almost fun. She bought Guy several ridiculously expensive fishing lures that Daniel swore he'd love. For Max, she bought the newest jazz CD. When Daniel asked how she knew Max liked jazz, Lace only winked at him, earning a scowl.

She even bought her mother a gift, a beautiful crystal vase, though they hadn't even acknowledged a holiday in too many years to count. Daniel stayed by her side, teasing and suggesting the most outrageous things. But when she bought a very sexy teddy for Annie, he'd stomped away, telling her he'd meet her at the food court. Lace used the private moment to buy Daniel's gifts, then fretted the rest of the afternoon over whether or not he'd like them.

"I need to stop at the post office. It's on the way to my place."

Daniel slanted her a quick glance. "I thought we'd go back to my place for a while."

It wasn't what he said, but how he said it, that caused her weariness to vanish, replaced by acute interest. She swallowed, then turned her head on the headrest to stare at him. "Oh? And what do we need to go there for?"

His hands flexed on the wheel, tightening, and she could see the movement of his jaw, the subtle way he shifted in his seat. "You're almost healed. Another few days and you'll be...fine."

Even though the snow continued to fall and the temperature was in the twenties, Lace felt too warm. She opened her dark cape and concentrated on breathing.

Daniel glanced at her again, and then continued. "I thought we could use today to...practice a little."

"To prepare for our nefarious plan?"

He reached across the seat and took her hand. "It's not nefarious. It's... Hell, I don't know what it is. I'm only a man, Lace. I can't take much more of this."

"Well, I'm a woman, and it hasn't exactly been easy on me."

"No?"

She shook her head. "I think about you all the time."

"When you're trying to work?"

She nodded and he said, "Me, too. When you're eating?"

"Yes."

His fingers tightened on hers. "When you're in bed?"

Her heart pounded, shaking her. "Especially then."

"Good. I'm glad."

"Misery loves company?"

"I haven't been miserable. I've been on pins and needles and grouchy and not at all myself. And to top it all off, the nurses at the hospital are acting so damn strange. Suddenly they're coming on to me in force. I can't go into the dining room without practically getting attacked. It's bizarre."

Uh-oh. Lace remembered prodding the nurse in the emergency room to be more aggressive in her pursuit. Thinking of it now, she realized what a petty, childish thing she had done. Not that she'd admit it to Daniel. "Hmm. Maybe your new sexuality is showing through, inspiring them all to greater daring."

"What are you talking about?"

"You've been friendlier with me, easier to be around."

He laughed. "Yeah, but you're the only one I ever wasn't friendly to."

"Gosh, that makes me feel so special."

His laughter stopped. He pulled her hand to his thigh and pressed his own over it. "You are special, Lace. I think that's why I had such a hard time understanding you. I've never met anyone like you before."

"You mean someone so brazen and unashamed?"

To her surprise, he seemed to seriously consider her words. "I'm afraid you'll take this the wrong way, so please let me finish." He paused, and she could see him visibly gather his thoughts. "You are brazen, but not in a bad way. You believe in what you say, in the work you do. I think that probably makes you more effective. And I know you're stronger than anyone I know, male or female. I've enjoyed helping you out while you were recuperating, but I have no doubt you'd have managed just as well on your own. Even without family or a hoard of friends.''

She'd never in her life heard so many compliments, not aimed at herself. He was wrong, of course. She wasn't strong, and her brazenness hid an insecurity, a fear of never finding love, of going through her entire life alone. Of being like her mother.

She didn't rely on friends because she'd never been comfortable enough with the natural intrusion of friends. People got close, and they wanted to share your life, invade your thoughts and dreams. His sister Annie, in her open, careless, honest way, had wheedled her way into her heart. She loved Annie as she'd love a sister if she had one. If she wasn't careful, she might begin to love the whole family.

''What are you thinking? You're so quiet.''

Lace quickly censored her thoughts, and decided which ones were safe to share. ''I was remembering how Annie and I met.''

''At Annie's bookstore?''

''Yes.'' Lace smiled, thinking of the quaint, conservative little bookstore Annie owned. It was located in a very exclusive neighborhood, on the same strip with several other specialty shops. ''She'd ordered a shipment of my last book. She saw in my bio that I lived in the area, so she wrote to my publisher, and they forwarded her letter.'' Lace grinned, giving Daniel's thigh a squeeze. ''She was most impressed with my prose.''

Daniel didn't take the bait. ''She's still young and impressionable.''

''She's in love.''

He almost drove the car off the road. ''What the hell are you talking about?''

"You didn't know? You haven't seen the signs? What do you do? Walk around with blinders on?"

They still tended to insult each other with great regularity, but neither one took the verbal assaults seriously. Not anymore. "Annie is only stretching her wings. She's not in love." He scoffed at the mere idea.

"Yes, she is. And that's why she wrote me. She read my book, and knew I'd understand her predicament."

"What predicament?"

"Being sandwiched between a serious older brother who pretends she's still a child, and an aggressive middle brother who growls if men even look her way."

"Max does that?"

"Max is as protective as you are, only in a different way. He's determined to browbeat any suitors away. And if that doesn't work, he'll just get physical."

Daniel narrowed his eyes. "I hadn't realized. About Max, I mean. Though I can picture him doing just that." He flashed her an unreadable look. "I still don't think Annie's in love."

"Think what you like. Doesn't matter to me."

"Okay, smartie. So, who's she in love with?"

Lace grinned. "I can't tell. It's a secret."

"Ha. You just don't have a name."

Caressing his thigh just enough to distract him, Lace leaned close and whispered, "Wait and see. I imagine the truth will come out soon enough."

As she'd hoped, he ignored her words and concentrated on her touch. "Will you come home with me, Lace?"

"What will you do to me?"

His jaw clenched and he shook. "Whatever you want me to."

She closed her eyes against the impact of his words. "What if I want to do things to you?"

He took his eyes off the road long enough to pull her up close and kiss her hard. Then he gently pushed her back to her own seat. "We can iron out the particulars when we get there. But in the meantime, do me a huge favor and withhold all further provocation. It's not necessary, believe me, and I have no idea how to perform CPR on myself. Much more of this and I'll expire with a heart attack."

Lace kept her words to herself. But her thoughts drifted, and before they reached his house, she felt certain she was in as bad a shape as Daniel. Maybe worse.

Seven

Daniel watched as Lace slowly pulled herself from the car. He was rushing things, pushing her too fast. She still needed time to heal, and today, with all the running around, she looked especially tired. Beautiful, but tired. He held her arm to make certain she wouldn't slip on the icy ground and looked down at her.

"This was a bad idea."

Lace reached up and smoothed her fingertips over his mouth. "Nonsense. It's an excellent idea. Don't be nervous."

His eyes widened. Lace thought he feared the idea of being intimate? What he feared was the depth of his feelings for her. It wasn't something he'd bargained for. Knowing she'd gone to another doctor to have her wound checked, then later to have the stitches removed, had outraged his possessive instincts. He didn't trust anyone else to care for her—and he didn't want anyone else looking at her body. Ridiculous, being that he was a doctor himself and understood the level of detachment between physician and patient.

Somehow it just didn't matter with Lace.

"You look ready to fall on your face. Have you taken a pain pill today?"

She scoffed. "I don't need them anymore. Honestly, Daniel, I'm fine. Quit clucking like a mother hen, take a deep breath and invite me in."

He succumbed to her suggestion. Of course, being that he was male and she was more beautiful and desirable than any woman he'd ever known, she might have stood silent and he'd have given in. He wanted her too much to wait.

A huge wreath decorated his front door, drawing Lace's attention. "You enjoy decorating for the holidays, don't you?"

He unlocked the door and pushed it open. "It's a tradition. My mother always had a wreath on every door, mistletoe in every doorway, and lights strung over everything that didn't move. Annie and Max can barely remember, but I do."

He held her hand as they stepped inside, then he kissed her, a light, teasing kiss that made her smile. He pointed toward the ceiling. "Mistletoe," he said.

Lace kicked the door closed with her small boot, took him by the collar of his coat, and pulled his mouth down to her own. "A real kiss," she whispered against his mouth.

Damn, but she could make his hair curl when she put her mind to it. Daniel tried to keep his hands at his sides, tried to moderate his breathing. But then her tongue touched his and he lost control. He pulled her gently closer, meshing their bodies together, instinctively pressing his groin into her soft belly. He ate at her mouth, loving the taste of her, and she moaned in approval.

"Lace…"

"Let's get out of our coats." He watched as she shrugged off her cape, letting it slip to the floor behind her. Dressed in her requisite black, she looked stunning. A black, hip-length cashmere sweater, black leggings, and black ankle boots made the paleness of her hair and the deep green of her eyes more pronounced.

She looked at him expectantly and he slipped his own coat off, draping it over an arm. He wanted to get out of everything, wanted her naked and open and anxious, but he had to play shy and timid. That took a lot of thought, so he used the time it took him to put their coats away to ponder the problem.

"Would you like some coffee?" Even as the words left his mouth, he winced. He sounded like a damned inane fool.

She blinked at him in lazy confusion. "Above all things, coffee was what I wanted."

He started to laugh, but turned it into a cough. Impatient little witch. "You can look around at the house if you like, while I get the coffee going."

To his surprise, she headed down the hall to the bedrooms. Daniel leaned around the corner and watched her.

"Which room is yours?"

His brain immediately conjured vivid images of her stripping naked, reposing herself on top of his patchwork quilt, arranging herself for his perusal. He shook his head. "The door at the very end of the hall. Along the way is the hall bath, my study and a spare room, in that order."

"Thanks." She disappeared into his bedroom, and curiosity got the better of him. He followed.

"What are you doing, Lace?"

"Just looking around, as you suggested. You've seen my bedroom, inspected my drawers and my underthings. It only seems fair that I have a peek, too."

"You intend to check out my briefs?"

"Hmm. Later, when you undress." Her eyes shown brightly with a mixture of nervousness and excitement. "But for now, I just wanted to see your house, to see if I come away as surprised as you did."

He barely registered her words; his brain had quit functioning when she mentioned watching him strip. "Lace, aren't you going a bit fast?"

She looked under his high, antique bed. Why, he had no idea. Did she think he hid girlie magazines there? Or maybe a girlie? Next, she peered into his closet.

"I'm only trying to catch up, Daniel." Her hands trembled as she rifled through his clothes. "Don't worry. I'm not rushing you."

"I wasn't worried."

She flashed him a quick, nervous smile. "Good. I want you to relax, to think of this as a natural thing."

"'This'?"

"Us being together. There's nothing to fear, you know. I'm not going to be judging your performance." Her cheeks pinkened and she cleared her throat. "As you said, we'll just get better acquainted with each other."

Crossing his arms behind his back, he leaned against the wall. He needed the physical support to remain upright. "I sort of figured we'd start in the living room, have a little conversation, maybe neck a little."

"I imagine we'll neck a lot." She tilted her head toward him. "You do like kissing, don't you? Even though you need some practice?"

"I like kissing."

"Excellent." She perched on the edge of his bed and bounced lightly, testing his mattress, he supposed. His vision fogged. "Soft enough. That's good."

He started to ask, *Soft enough for what?* but couldn't seem to force the words from his mouth, not with Lace leaning down to tug off her boots. Then he noticed the slight frown of pain her movements caused her, and he went to her.

"Let me do that."

Kneeling, he took her small foot onto his lap and pulled off her boot. Lace took his actions in stride, leaning back onto her elbows on his bed and watching him with an interested gaze. After he'd pulled off the second boot, he stood. "Comfy?"

"I'm getting there."

Her voice had dropped a little and the pink flush staining her cheeks spread to her throat. Arousal. His knees nearly buckled. He wanted to step between her legs and lower his body onto hers, to press his hard frame into her soft one. He wanted to ride her gently until she cried out, then ride her hard until they were both insensate. Instead, he sat beside her on the mattress and tried to look uncertain. The effort sorely taxed him.

"Are you sure you don't want any coffee?"

She took several fast, shallow breaths, then shook her head. "I want you."

His eyes closed and he swallowed. If he moved, he'd blow everything. He hadn't counted on the effect of her words, of her desire. He couldn't do this, couldn't pretend a distance he didn't feel, not when every muscle in his body strained for her, not when he felt harder than he ever had in his entire life.

The bed dipped as Lace sat up. He felt his glasses

slide off as she removed them, then the cool, soft touch of her mouth on each eyelid. Evidently she'd taken his hesitation for reserve and was determined to encourage him.

"Number one, Daniel. There's nothing to be embarrassed about." Her voice was soft, breathy. "Anything we do together, anything we find mutually satisfying, is good."

His fingers knotted in the quilt to keep from touching her. He kept his eyes closed. Lace leaned across him to put his glasses on the nightstand, then caught the hem of his sweater and worked it up his body.

"I love how you look, Daniel." He obediently raised his arms when she nudged him, and the sweater skimmed over his head. Lace tossed it aside and then smoothed his hair back into place, petting him, but not where he'd like, not where he desperately wanted her touch.

Her knuckles brushed his belly when she began working on his belt and he groaned, a ragged, hoarse sound. His body shook with the restraint put on it, and matched the nervous shaking of her hands.

With her lips touching his ear, Lace whispered, "Lean back."

When he didn't do so quickly enough to suit her, she pressed her hands to his shoulders and urged him backward. He went, but she went with him, landing on his chest with a soft sigh. He felt her hair sweep down to tickle his cheekbones as she touched her mouth to his. Her hands coasted over his shoulders, then his chest, lightly striking over his nipples. He pressed his head back into the mattress and tried to think of other things, of the hospital, the snow outside. Lace kissed his throat.

"You're so tight. Relax a little."

His rough laugh showed her how ludicrous he thought that suggestion to be.

Then she went back to his belt.

Out of sheer preservation, Daniel caught her hands. "Lace, wait." He didn't recognize his own voice.

"Shh. It's all right. I won't hurt you."

That bit of inanity nearly pushed him over the edge. Enough was enough. If she didn't slow down, he wouldn't last, wouldn't be able to give her pleasure, and more than anything, more than his own need, he wanted to see Lace McGee in the throes of a climax.

He carried each of her small fists to his mouth and kissed them. "Don't you have some catching up to do?"

When she lifted a brow, he touched the edge of her sweater, then saw her cheeks darken with color as understanding dawned.

"You...you want me to take my clothes off?"

Her nervous response was endearing, especially in light of how hard she'd been working to relax him, to put him at ease. "Don't you want to?" he asked, managing to inject just enough insecurity into his question to prompt her to action.

"Sure. All right." If anything, she looked even more uncertain, and he wondered at it. Perhaps she had a special way of doing things, a certain organization to her seduction. Maybe disrobing was supposed to come later, but he needed to have access to her now, to touch and taste her so that they'd both be in the same boat, so to speak. When he drowned, he wanted her with him.

Lace turned her back and wiggled out of her sweater, taking her time about it. Daniel admired the smooth line of her back, the dip of her waist, the flare of her hips. She had one tiny mole on the top of her right shoulder blade, and he leaned forward to kiss it. Lace froze.

Warily looking over her shoulder at him, she asked, "Well? Shouldn't you be getting your shoes off?"

He didn't understand her rush. To Daniel, most of the pleasure in lovemaking was taking his time, enjoying a woman's body, playing with her, teasing. Letting the tension build until they were both crazy with need. Lace seemed to be moving at Mach speed for some reason. He wondered if his supposed inexperience made her nervous, or if she assumed he was the one in a hurry.

Maybe she even thought he'd back down if she didn't race through things.

He smiled at her. "If that's what you want. You're the one in charge here, remember."

She unhooked the front closure of her bra—a snowy white, lacy affair that surprised him as much as it pleased him. She held the cups to her chest and kept her back turned to him. Despite his building urgency, he shrugged, willing to let her call the shots.

When he leaned over to yank off his shoes and socks, Lace draped herself across his back and hugged him. The shock of feeling her soft, full breasts against his skin made him shudder. He started to turn to her, but she held him tight. "Shh. Relax, Daniel."

He wished she'd quit telling him that. Relaxation at this point was as beyond him as the moon.

Smoothing her palms up and down his skin, she let her nipples graze his back again and again until he knew he'd explode if she didn't stop. It would all be over with, and Lace would be assured of his inept abilities. He grit his teeth and forced her to release him as he turned.

Her gaze moved away as he looked at her. She was so damned sexy, so beautiful. It was his turn to press her back onto the mattress, and she allowed it, closing her eyes and biting her lips. Daniel stripped her leggings off her with one long tug, taking her matching white bikini panties at the same time. Lace turned her face away, until her nose almost touched the mattress. But since his attention wasn't centered on her nose, he dismissed her actions and took in the beauty of her body.

She wasn't perfect, as he'd always thought, but the narrowness of her hips excited him, as did the slight swell of her belly. Beneath her breasts he could see her ribs and he thought she needed to gain some weight, but her legs, long and lightly muscled and smooth, made it impossible to draw a deep breath.

The curly tangle of hair between her thighs was pale and silky, and he smiled. A true blonde.

Belatedly remembering his plan, he whispered, ''I want to kiss you, Lace.''

Her eyes shot open, caught the direction of his gaze, and she gasped. ''Where?''

Everywhere. ''Wherever you'd like.''

She licked her lips and a frown of concentration puckered her brow. Finally, after an undue amount of thought and an audible swallow, she touched her breast. ''Here.''

Daniel laid his hand gently on her breast, then watched her belly hollow out as she sucked in her breath. Slowly, letting her anticipate his touch, he circled her nipple with one fingertip. Her nipple puckered, and the pale pink turned rosier. Lightly, he pinched, and she twisted, curling in on a low sound of pleasure.

Never had he been so aroused over so little, but seeing Lace's free response nearly broke his restraint. He leaned down and licked her, one slow stroke of his tongue. ''Here?''

Her breathing turned raspy, and she nodded.

He kissed her, a small, lighter-than-air touch, then asked, ''You're certain?''

''Yes!'' She gripped his head and pressed him closer.

Smiling, he took her deep into his mouth and sucked tenderly. Lace tangled her fingers in his hair and held him tight, one of her long legs snagging his hips and pulling his body close. She groaned and whimpered, and her reaction fueled his own.

He kissed her other breast, then jerked free to shove off his pants. Lace watched him through wide, glazed eyes. He lowered himself back to her side and cupped her mound, tangling his fingers in her soft, curly hair. She arched against him, breathless, trembling. ''Daniel, please.''

''Tell me what to do.'' No longer playing the novice, he asked out of a sense of seduction, knowing the question would arouse her further, would allow her to keep that impression of control.

''Touch me.'' The words were said on a moan, and Daniel complied.

His fingers pressed, parted. The soft sounds coming from deep in her throat encouraged him.

''Open your legs a little, sweetheart.''

The second her thighs parted, he slipped his finger in, not deep, just teasing, testing her readiness. To his surprise and immense pleasure, she was wet, hot, swelled. And incredibly tight. He groaned with her.

They each seemed to have forgotten their roles, and Daniel had no intention of reminding her. He could barely think, barely breathe; he sure as hell couldn't act!

Lace's hips lifted in tandem with the movements of his hand and suddenly it was too much. He turned away to retrieve a condom from the nightstand, and he no sooner had it on, than Lace was reaching for him, her fingers digging deep into the muscles of his shoulders, urging him to haste.

A single second of clarity righted in his mind, and he clasped Lace's hips, remembering her injury. "Onto your side, sweetheart."

She froze, then stared at him.

"I don't want to hurt you, Lace." His words were hushed, hurried. "It'll be easier on you this way. I can control things better."

She frowned, her eyes momentarily darkening in suspicion, but he didn't give her a chance to think about this evidence of his experience. He turned her to face him, then brought her uninjured leg over his hip.

Lace stared at him wide-eyed, confused, anxious, curious. He wanted to bury himself in her, make her a part of him, but he'd noticed the still pink scar on her bottom, an angry reminder of her delicate condition. Daniel touched it lightly with his fingertips, soothing her, then summoned the last of nearly lost reserve and entered her gently, measuring her, clenching his jaw at the tightness of her, the natural resistance of her body. He saw Lace squeeze her eyes closed, saw her soft lips part as she drew in a long shuddering breath. Her shoulders grew taut, her back arched as she pushed her hips toward him.

By small degrees, he went deeper, trying to moderate his movements, trying to protect her from the violence of his lust. He moved one hand to her belly and caressed her, smiling at her small cry of excitement.

Her feminine muscles squeezed him, holding him so tight. *Too tight,* as if she'd never been touched this way before. And in the space of a heartbeat, realization hit and he lost his breath in one loud whoosh.

"Lace?" He stared at her flushed face and waited for the world to right itself.

Her arms slid up to tighten around his neck and she pressed her cheek into his throat. "This…" She swal-

lowed, and he could feel the slight movements of her
body, the way she tried to remain still but couldn't.
"This is a…a *bad* time for talking, Daniel."

"But you're a *virgin?*" He tried to dip his head, to
see her face, but she kept her expression hidden. A virgin? His mind couldn't simulate the consequences of
such an occurrence. He stared at her tumbled hair, at her
trembling shoulders, and he felt something strange,
something warm and insistent and deep invade his soul.
It curled in his chest, squeezing him, making his vision
cloud with emotion, making his heart ache.

"Yes, Daniel, I'm aware of that." She sounded ragged, her voice trembling. "It would be a difficult thing
for me to miss."

Damn difficult for him to miss, too. Why hadn't she
told him? Various reasons presented themselves, but he
couldn't seem to grasp a single one. "Lace…"

"Not *now*, Daniel!"

She moved, pressing back against him, demanding his
attention—*as if she didn't already have it.* And he
groaned, rational thought completely beyond him, his
wits successfully scattered by the tight, rhythmic clasp
of her body. He held her hips and thrust himself completely into her, reveling in her groans, her awkward
attempts to counter his movements.

No man had ever held her this way. No man had ever
touched her as he had.

The truth pounded through his brain, through his
heart. His body seemed to pulse with physical and emotional sensations, combining to destroy his strength and
thought. On some subconscious level, he remained
aware of her recent hurts and moderated his thrusts, careful not to add to her injury. She cried out, first in low
groans, then increasing, each sound, each small whim-

per, driving him higher until he knew he wouldn't last, until he was lost and there was no hope for it, no pulling back.

He covered her breasts with his palms, lightly bit her shoulder and muffled his hoarse shout against her soft, fragrant skin as he shuddered out his release.

After a moment his weight caused her to collapse. Daniel rolled onto his back, his arms wide, his legs numb, his body still pulsing in pleasurable throbs of aftershock.

He became aware of Lace moving beside him, of her watching him curiously. "You're not going to do something stupid like fall asleep, are you?"

Grinning was a feat requiring more strength than he presently owned. "No. Rest."

Lace smacked his shoulder. "Why did you quit?"

He cocked one eye open and found her looming over him. "I was done." He meant *done for,* shot, incapable of breathing, much less moving, but she didn't take it that way.

She leaned down until her nose almost touched his. "Well, I wasn't done!"

"I know. Sorry." He closed his eyes, fighting the urge to laugh. "Let me catch my breath and I'll show the…depth of my atonement for leaving you."

"Humph!"

She started to leave the bed, but he caught her arm and tugged her back down. "Don't be angry, Lace. I said I'll make it up to you."

"How?"

"Don't look at me as if I have evil intents on your fair person." Now he did chuckle. The absurd humor of the situation did much to revive him. She scowled, started to speak, and he kissed her. A real kiss, using all his expertise, intent on showing her just how good they could be together.

And Lace, unfulfilled, her body still warm and trembling, melted like an ice cube in the August sun.

Daniel kissed her until she clutched at him, until her nails dug into his flesh, until her body moved against his in need. He slid down her body, to her breasts and her still rosy, puckered nipples. He nipped and licked and praised her for her deep, throaty moans, given without artifice, without holding back. His tongue flicked over the tip of her nipple and she cried out, pulling him closer. He suckled her until her hips jerked upward, seeking him, her need as strong as his own.

''You're so beautiful, Lace.''

This time she didn't tease him about the compliment. She whimpered, her body damp with a fine sheen of sweat. He kissed her belly and she writhed beneath him as he moved lower, lower. When he parted her with his thumbs and covered her with his mouth, she returned his praise in breathless words and seductive sounds, begging for more, and he gave it to her.

Without hesitation, in halting gasps, she told him what she liked, and in the middle of a muttered, nearly incoherent sentence of unnecessary instruction, she reached her peak, gasping, her body taut and her scent strong. She gave a muffled scream, and he loved it, thrilled with her response, and his obvious success. Daniel held her steady and continued to kiss and lick and stroke her until she went limp and her moans faded to soft, satisfied sighs.

He'd never taken so much pleasure in his ability to make love. He felt like crowing, like writing his own damn book—which could sit beside Lace's on the shelf. He gathered her close and stroked her back, her injured bottom. He felt the edge of the scar there, and wanted to kiss it. He kissed her open mouth instead, and smiled when she didn't so much as pucker. Breathing seemed to require all her concentration.

He was almost asleep, his brain finally at rest since the first time he'd met her, his body appeased, when suddenly Lace leaned up and her small fist thumped hard against his chest.

Here we go again, he thought, and opened his eyes in question.

"You miserable fraud! You rotten cretin! You know exactly what you're about, don't you?"

His chest swelled with pride; he felt like the Cheshire cat, his grin was so huge. "Actually, yes, I have been known to gain a compliment or two."

Her eyes narrowed to mere slits and she started to hit him again, but he caught her wrist. "Stop that. You'll hurt yourself."

Her eyes nearly crossed in her rage. "Dammit, Daniel—"

He interrupted, energy surging back into his body. "What about you, Lace? A damned *virgin?* I almost had heart failure!"

"So why didn't you?"

She didn't mean it, he thought, feeling his own annoyance grow. "If you want to know, I was too busy listening to you beg me to—"

She slapped her hand over his mouth. "I never begged."

He grinned, removing her hand. "Yeah, you did. And I enjoyed every word."

She jerked away from him. "Don't change the subject, Daniel. You lied to me."

True enough, but as far as he was concerned, the point

was moot at this stage. He didn't want to fight. "Lace, we've both been less than honest, don't you think?"

"I never lied to you! You drew your own ridiculous conclusions. But you deliberately deceived me."

Leaning up on one elbow, he growled, "My conclusions weren't that ridiculous based on how you behaved around me. You came on to me constantly, Lace, with no show of discretion, despite the fact you knew I didn't want you."

"Ha! You wanted me all right. At least be honest about that."

He couldn't very well deny it, given that even now, he was getting hard again. They were on top of the quilt, both naked, and his renewed interest was more than obvious if the woman bothered to look down. He shrugged. "Yeah, but I did my best to hide it."

"Now that's a fact I know all too well." She looked at him with distaste. "You spend so much time hiding, from yourself and everyone else, it's a wonder your patients can ever find you."

"At least I own an ounce or two of propriety."

"Which translated, means I do not? Well, let me tell you something, *Danny*. I may have encouraged your stupid assumptions, but only because you made me so mad, always acting like you were better than me."

Quietly, his guilt strong, he said, "I never said that."

"But you thought it. It scares you to death that Annie and I are friends."

He felt lost, no sensible argument coming to his aid. Going on the defensive seemed his only recourse, and he did, summoning up his best show of umbrage. "Lace, how can you possibly be a virgin?"

"Simple." She curled her lip in a credible sneer and glared at him. "All I've ever met are jerks like you."

"So why did you sleep with me, Lace?" As he spoke, he trailed his fingertips down her arm and watched goose bumps rise in the wake. Ha! Regardless of what the woman would like him to believe, she wasn't immune to him. Not by a long shot.

That fact filled him with intense male satisfaction.

Lace scooted off the bed, then pulled back the coverlet and climbed beneath, pulling it up to her chin. Daniel enjoyed her antics, consoling himself over the loss of her nudity by the fact that she hadn't left the room or even the bed. She'd only grown tired of his overly interested gaze.

Sighing, he came to his feet beside the bed. He felt Lace watching him, her gaze warm and full of curiosity. He was still half hard, but he supposed they had to talk before they could proceed further.

The late afternoon light barely shone through his frost-covered window. Outside, a tree branch heavy with snow scraped the side of the house, moved by the winter wind. And in his bed, huddled under his covers with an adorable show of belated modesty, was the most appealing, most complex and intriguing woman he'd ever met. He stood by the side of the bed and slipped on his glasses; he wanted to see her clearly, to make certain he didn't miss a single thing about this very special moment in time. Then he propped his hands on his naked hips.

Lace's gaze skittered away, then back again. She licked her lips. "Why don't you put something on?"

"Answer my question, Lace."

Tightening her grip on the quilt, she glared up at him in defiance. "Why shouldn't I have slept with you?" She waved a dismissive hand at his body. "You're available, attractive and even you had to have noticed the sexual chemistry between us."

"I'm not buying it, sweetheart."

"Don't call me that."

"You didn't complain earlier."

Heat blossomed in her cheeks. "I wasn't myself then."

Laughing, he sat on the edge of the bed and flicked the tip of her nose. "Whoever you were, I liked you. Hell, I still like you. Don't you like me just a bit?"

"No."

"Tsk, tsk. You shouldn't lie, Lace. A few hours ago I might have believed you. But not now. Now I know just how discriminating you've been all your life. And I know a little thing like sexual chemistry wouldn't have changed anything if you'd truly despised me."

"Well, there's where you're wrong. I'd never felt it before, so how could I help but respond to it?"

He wondered if she had any idea how her words affected him, how territorial they made him feel. He moved closer to her, propping his back on the headboard and tugging her close despite her resistance. "Just let me hold you, Lace. That is what men and women do after sex, you know." He paused, struck by his words. "Come to think of it, you wouldn't know, would you? But it's true. They hold each other."

"Not always." She tried to wiggle away, but when he held on, she relented and plopped back against him. "I know more about sex than you ever will, Daniel. I've been studying it my entire adult life. And what you say isn't at all true. Sometimes, after sex, the man just gets up and walks away."

"Or the woman."

She shrugged, a nonverbal agreement.

Daniel enjoyed the feel of her at his side, the plump softness of her breast pressed into his ribs, the silkiness of her hair against his chin. He kissed her crown and breathed in her scent.

He was aware of her thinking, considering everything that had happened. He didn't know what conclusions she'd drawn, and it bothered him. "Lace?"

Her sigh was one of disgust. "Honesty forces me to admit that there are a few select times when I suppose I like you a little."

He burst out laughing. "So fulsome with your compliments." She leaned her cheek against his chest and his arms tightened. "Well? When do you like me? Or is the situation so rare, you can't even remember anymore?"

"I remember." Her voice had turned soft, gentle. "When you're with Annie. You're so careful with her and it's obvious how much you care for her, how close the two of you are. It's a wonderful thing to witness. And Max, how you deal with him, though sometimes you are so blind I want to smack you. But other times, I can see how Max respects you, and he's a good man, mostly because of you."

He felt touched to his soul by her praise.

"Sometimes when I'm at the hospital with my own work, or meeting Annie there, I see you with a patient, and you have that intense, concentrated look on your face because you care so much."

Here she was, waxing eloquent on his sterling character, and he thought of all the times he'd put her down, judged her harshly. He'd been an idiot, a complete fool.

And he'd dug himself into a hole so deep, it would take him a while to work his way out.

His hand smoothed over her hip, toward her bottom. "I didn't hurt you, did I?"

Her nose bumped his nipple as she shook her head. "No. I'm fine."

"Lace?" He wanted her again, right now, this time with no games between them. He cupped her chin and started to tilt her face up. But she slipped away.

"Oh, no, you don't. I'm still mad at you, Dr. Sawyers. What you did was reprehensible. Will you take me home, or should I call a cab?"

Eight

"Do you see Santa Claus out there, or are you just avoiding Daniel?"

Lace turned, smiling at Guy Donovan as he stepped up beside her at the dark window. She'd been staring out, daydreaming, feeling vaguely discontent. She welcomed the interruption to her thoughts. "It's a beautiful sight, with all the snow on the trees and the twinkling lights everywhere. I love Daniel's house, especially how it's situated here among all the trees."

Daniel's house had a homey, lived-in look, for a bachelor. The furniture, though dark and heavy, was comfortable and functional. And he'd hung prints on all the walls and set photos of his family everywhere. The house was one floor with a large basement and a spacious yard that abutted the woods in back and a narrow creek on one side; it was a house meant for a family, for kids.

Resting his long lanky body against the wall, Guy crossed his arms over his chest and studied her. "This house is fine. But Daniel should have kept his family home after his father moved out, instead of me living there. But the memories are too tough for him to deal with."

"I know." Daniel had already explained to her that Guy agreed to live in the family home, since Annie and Max had both taken apartments, and Daniel didn't want it. And like Daniel, his father avoided the house and the memories. All too often, it seemed, he avoided his children as well. Any reminder of his wife, especially at the holidays, was more than he wanted to deal with. Lace understood that, and how difficult it was for Daniel. "Daniel remembers his mother better than Max or Annie do."

"I remember her, too," Guy said. "She was a fantastic lady. Unlike Daniel, I like the reminders, seeing little things every day that bring back the memories. They're good memories. I practically grew up in that house, and I think it's important to keep it around, for Annie's and Max's sake."

"You and Daniel have been friends a long time."

A smile spread over Guy's face, and for the first time Lace noticed how handsome he was. With his ruthlessly short hair, rangy walk and sloppy attire, he'd always seemed inconspicuous enough.

Even now, at Daniel's Christmas get-together, Guy was dressed in a loose flannel shirt over a faded gray T-shirt with jeans that had seen better days. And his hair, short as it was, still managed to stick out at odd angles.

He ran his hand over that hair, demonstrating for Lace how such a style was possible, then nodded. "We've known each other since grade school. He's like a brother to me.'' His gaze scanned the room beyond them, and as Annie came into sight, her snug red dress hugging the curves of her body, Lace saw Guy stiffen and scowl.

Distracted, keeping his gaze on Annie, he muttered, ''The Sawyers are like family, Max and Annie included.''

Annie laughed at something Max said, swatted at her brother and moved out of view.

Guy gave his attention back to Lace. ''I'm glad you came today. Annie enjoys your company and she needs more friends, to get out more often. She's been kind of strange lately.''

Despite her resolve to forget Daniel's perfidy, Lace asked, ''You're not worried about me corrupting her?''

''Annie? Ha! She has a will of iron and more stubbornness than her two brothers combined. Even as a baby, she could get her way on any and every little thing. No, Annie will always do exactly as she pleases, and she couldn't possibly be influenced by anyone to be other than what she wants to be. Usually a pain in the neck.''

Lace looked back out the window. Snow on Christmas Day was supposed to be a magical thing. She felt anything but magical. Since that ill-fated day when she and Daniel had made love, she hadn't been able to think straight. She wanted to stay away from him, because she knew he was dangerous, both to her heart and her beliefs.

But he'd made her feel things she'd never imagined, and she wanted to feel them again. Even now, being in his home and hearing the music, the laughter and easy, casual conversation, made her crave things she had never wanted before. She wondered where her mother was, what she was doing and who she was with. She wondered if her mother had liked the vase, or if she'd even gotten the gift yet.

Lace swallowed and took another sip of her punch. Without her mind's permission, the words came out. "Daniel doesn't want me anywhere around his sister. He doesn't even want me around Max."

Guy tilted his head, considering that. "He's always been overprotective of Annie. He lost his mother, and he's afraid of losing her, too. Plus, he doesn't think any man is good enough for her, and he can't quite reconcile himself to the fact that Annie has grown up, that she's a woman now, and men might want her. It's easier to blame you than to accept that things are changing. As far as Max is concerned, he's just jealous."

Lace nearly dropped her cup of punch. "Jealous? Why in heaven's name would he be jealous of Max?"

"Lace." Guy shook his head, looking down at her with a chastising frown. "You're not naive. You have to know Daniel wants you. But he thinks Max wants you, too. Hell, he thinks every man wants you, and it makes him nuts. That's the main reason he's so rude, you know. Not because he doesn't like you, but because he doesn't want every other man liking you."

Lace thought about the possibility of what he said. Obviously Guy had no idea that she and Daniel had already gotten past the hostility, however brief their truce had been. How could he know? Since that day, they'd hardly spoken without bickering. Daniel was irritated that she wouldn't see the reasoning behind his deception—even though he hadn't given her a good reason. And Lace simply wanted to avoid losing herself to a man who disdained her very existence, who was ashamed to admit he wanted her.

"Come on. Brooding over here in the corner isn't going to prove anything. And Annie is starting to give us worried glances. Besides, if you hide over here too long, Max will join you and try to steal a kiss, which will provoke Daniel just as Max. hopes it will, and they'll start arguing. Christmas will be ruined.''

Lace laughed. ''So I have the power to single-handedly ruin a holiday for the entire family? I don't think so.''

''I know so.'' Guy took her arm and herded her back to the living room. Lace felt like a shrimp beside him, he was so tall, a good three or four inches taller than Daniel and Max, who shared a similar height of six feet.

Daniel called everyone to dinner and Guy played the gallant, seating her next to him. Annie sat across from Guy, and Daniel and Max took opposite seats at the head and foot of the table.

They were still serving themselves when Max said, ''Heard your show last night, Lace.''

She scooped up a serving of mashed potatoes and passed on the bowl. Without looking up, she said, ''That was a fun one, wasn't it?''

''I thought so.'' Then Max added, ''And damned sexy.''

''I wanted to do something a little more lighthearted for the holidays.''

Guy handed her the platter of ham, then joined in. ''I heard it, too. I loved the fellow who told how he'd met his wife in the back of a taxi they'd shared on Christmas Eve, both of them rushing to get a last-minute gift.''

Annie leaned forward. ''I heard that! It was so funny. Imagine practically making love to a stranger in a taxi!''

The sound of a chair scraping back drew everyone's attention. Daniel stood there, glaring at Lace. ''Excuse me.''

He walked out of the room, stiff-legged and stone-faced. Lace threw down her napkin, muttering to herself.

Max burst out laughing. "God, he's got it bad. I wish I could get him to listen to one of your shows, Lace. Imagine his reaction."

Lace turned her narrowed gaze on him. "He's never even listened?"

Annie reached across the table to pat her hand. "Now, Lace. You know how he is. Don't let it bother you."

Guy just pursed his mouth and looked thoughtful.

"I should probably go. Daniel obviously doesn't feel comfortable and I feel like an intruder."

Vehement rebuttals followed her statement until Daniel reentered and calmly set a bowl on the table. He scanned the group, his eyes finally landing on Lace, his expression once more composed. "I forgot the sweet potatoes."

Max chuckled. "Can't have Christmas dinner without sweet potatoes."

Other than the music in the background, silence reigned while everyone finished serving themselves and began to eat. Guy endeared himself to Lace for all time when he reopened the conversation.

"I've listened to quite a few of your shows, Lace, and I think you do a fantastic job. It always amazes me how many people call in, and how open you are about things, making them comfortable, giving them someone to talk to when they have no one else."

Annie glanced at her brother, then lifted her chin. "She does a great service. Even the show last night, though it didn't concentrate on problems, gave people a chance to remember how they'd felt when they fell in love for the first time. One man said he and his wife had been arguing about how expensive the holidays have gotten and how much she'd spent, when your show came on. Then he got to thinking, remembering when they'd met and all they'd been through, and instead of arguing, they...well...'' Annie blushed, her gaze going to Guy. "You know."

Lace sighed. "They made love. I know. Too often people forget what is important and get wrapped up in the little things that annoy. It's all too easy to forget your priorities."

Max nodded, trying to look serious. "Like making love."

Exasperated, Daniel threw a spoon at him. "Will you knock it off?" But it was obvious he wasn't really angry because he chuckled. "You're such a damned reprobate, Max."

"It's my most redeeming quality."

They all laughed and after that, conversation resumed at a normal level. Lace stayed quiet, wishing herself elsewhere, anywhere other than in the midst of this family camaraderie. She felt out of place, and very uncomfortable. Fearing she might start another squabble, she simply stayed quiet and ate. Several times she felt Daniel watching her, but she refrained from looking at him, giving all her attention to the removal of the walnuts from her fruit salad.

When they all returned to the living room to open gifts, Lace tried to sidle off to a corner alone, but somehow she ended up sandwiched on the couch between Annie and Max. Guy sat on the floor across from them and Daniel passed out presents.

Max was incorrigible, shaking every gift, making wild guesses about what might be inside. Annie and Guy ridiculed him, saying he'd be lucky to get more than a lump of coal.

After all the presents were dispersed, Daniel held up an arm, gave them all a huge smile, then dropped his hand as if signaling a race. The unwrapping began, and Lace, who'd had visions of a very dignified display, laughed hysterically at the frenzied ripping of silver paper and colorful ribbons.

Annie "oohed" over her teddy, then held it up to show the others. Max cursed, Guy's ears turned red and Daniel cast a frown at Lace.

Lace waited, on edge as the others opened presents. But her fears were unfounded. Max cheered over his jazz CD and Guy launched a sermon on the type of fish to be won with his new lures. Lace was relieved by their apparent satisfaction of her gifts and her insecurity was put to rest.

She sat there smiling, pleased with herself, until Max nudged her to open her own gifts. Tentative, Lace opened her gift from Max. Inside a sturdy box, nestled in tissue paper, she found a sculpted kitten of colorful carnival glass. The kitten frolicked, rolling itself playfully around a shiny ball. Lace bit her lip and thought of the perfect place to put the treasure, in the window over her kitchen sink where the sunlight would pour through it.

"It's beautiful, Max. Thank you."

Max grinned at her, looking almost bashful, and for the first time, she gave him a kiss. He pretended to swoon, much to Daniel's disgust.

"Now mine." Guy prodded his present toward her. She hadn't realized that everyone else had finished with their gifts, their enthusiasm making the process speedy in comparison with her restraint. She pulled the ribbon aside and carefully unfolded the paper. She found a beautiful selection of pastel-colored stationery bordered with flowers, her initials embossed on the top in bright, elegant script.

She ran her fingers over the lettering and then smiled. ''Oh, Guy, it's perfect.''

''So glad you like it. I know you do a lot of correspondence.''

She accepted Guy's hug and did her best to ignore the way Daniel scrutinized her reactions. She didn't want anyone to know how emotionally touched she was by the gifts. She didn't want them to know how needy she suddenly felt.

Annie dropped a package in her lap. ''Mine next. Come on, Lace, you're so slow.''

Lace laughed, wiped at her eyes and, to please Annie, ripped the paper away. She eased her gift from the box, and it unfolded into an incredible mobile of crystal birds in every color. Fifteen birds hung suspended from gold chains at various levels. ''Oh, Annie.'' Almost breathless, Lace searched for words. ''It's…it's…'' She bit her lip and shook her head.

Annie laughed at her surprise, and they hugged each other, laughing and crying, oblivious to the indulgent male smiles surrounding them.

''My turn.'' Daniel picked up a large flat package, two feet by three feet. Annie scrambled to get the other presents from Lace and pile them together. When Daniel set the package in her lap, Lace blinked at the weight of it.

''Careful. It's fragile.''

Lace couldn't begin to imagine what it might be and she hesitated, looking at Daniel and feeling shocked at the tenderness in his eyes. She licked her lips and Max nudged her.

''Don't leave us in suspense. Get the thing open.''

Teasing herself, Lace pulled away a corner of the paper, peeked inside, then covered it again. Her hand went to her throat and she blinked at all of them.

"What is it?" Annie asked.

Guy leaned forward. "Yeah, what did he get you?"

"It's too much."

Daniel shook his head. "I thought it was suitable."

"Oh, it is. But Daniel, it's…"

"Open the damn thing," Max complained.

Daniel nodded, encouraging her, watching closely to see her reaction, and Lace took a deep breath. She peeled back the paper and a beautiful, oak-framed stained glass appeared. The colorful glass was arranged in an exquisite profusion of spring flowers, delicately crafted, so many colors intertwined and complementing each other that even Guy and Max stared in wonder. Lace's black sweater and slacks made a dramatic backdrop for the brightness of the glass as she held it balanced on her lap.

Lace knew it was an artist's piece, not a factory product. She could barely breathe, it was so beautiful, and so perfect. Already, she wanted to see it with the sunshine glowing through it, over it. She imagined it hanging in her bedroom, the many colors floating across her rainbow bed in the morning, brightening her day. She laid it flat on her lap.

Burying her face in her hands, she burst into tears.

She wasn't sure how it happened, but suddenly there was a lot of shuffling and murmuring and she was alone in the room with Daniel and he was lifting the glass carefully away from her. His arms went around her and he hushed her with whispered words. "It's all right, Lace."

She shook her head. She felt like an idiot, started to say so and hiccuped instead. "How did they all know?"

"That you like color?"

She nodded.

"I don't think they're all as stupid as I am. They know you, Lace. They care about you."

That made her cry harder. She didn't want them to care about her. Did she?

Daniel handed her his hankie. "I hope these are tears of happiness, that you're not considering breaking the glass over my hard head."

"And ruin my gift? No, I wouldn't do that."

"I'm glad." He rubbed her back. "You know, you scared poor Annie to death."

"I'm sorry." Lace buried her face in his shoulder and refused to surface. She felt shamed to her very bones at her ridiculous display and didn't want to face anyone, much less Daniel.

"No reason to be sorry. Annie shuffled everyone into the kitchen to help with coffee. Max and Guy probably think it's your time of the month or something."

Lace slugged him in the stomach for that male-inspired observation, and he grunted, then grabbed her fist and flattened it on his thigh. "Be fair, Lace. To the average man, that's a thing of mystery. Men feel safe accounting all excessive female displays on a woman being womanly."

"The average man? I take it you're excluding yourself from that category?"

"I'm a doctor. Of course I'm exempt."

"I love my gift, Daniel. Thank you."

He cupped the back of her head and tilted her face up. When she allowed it, he wiped at the tears on her cheeks. "It feels so damn good to hold you again, Lace. You've made me miserable these past few days."

"Good."

A smile tilted his mouth. "You like it that I was unhappy?"

"I like it that I wasn't the only one feeling horrible."

He kissed her, but when they heard the conversation in the kitchen, he broke away.

"Does your family know we're...involved?"

Stroking her cheek with his thumb, he smoothed away a new tear and smiled. "Nah. They figured I was the most qualified to deal with your hysteria, so they ran like the cowards they are and left me to fend for myself."

Mortification had her hiding her face again. "This is awful. I'm so embarrassed."

"I'm sorry. I shouldn't tease you." He kissed her temple and then set her away from him. "They know you well enough, Lace, to know you're usually alone on the holidays. And they know how emotional this time of the year is for everyone. No one thinks anything of it."

Running her fingers through her hair in an attempt to straighten it, Lace considered what to do next. She couldn't quite bring herself to look at Daniel.

"Would you like to help me pick up all this paper, then we can join everyone else?"

"Do you think they really liked my gifts? I wasn't sure..."

"Yes, *they* did. Very much"

Hearing the emphasis on "they," Lace grinned. She'd deliberately held his gift back, not wanting him to open it in front of everyone. "I have something for you, Daniel. But you have to wait until later."

His gaze darkened and he looked at her mouth with interest. "I hope it's what I'm thinking."

She laughed. "Well, it's not, so stop thinking it."

"Go away with me, Lace."

Her heart skipped a beat. "What?"

"Go away with me." He took her hands and held them close. "I know you have some time off now. Annie told me you're on vacation until after the first of the year. I am, too. Go away with me."

She stared at him, her body already heating in anticipation and her stomach growing tight. She carefully considered her response. "Go away, where?"

"I have a cabin. We could go there."

"I've never heard anything about a cabin."

"That's because I've told very few people about it."

"Wait a minute." A horrible suspicion began to gnaw on her brain and she glowered. "Why would you be secretive about the cabin?"

He looked away, then back again. "It just seemed appropriate, Lace."

Her eyes narrowed. "Is this some secret bachelor's cabin where you conduct your little liaisons? Is this where you gained all that damned experience you used against me?"

He frowned. "Lower your voice. And I didn't use anything against you, dammit. I gave you pleasure."

"Ha! Answer my question. Is this where you take women you have affairs with so that your reputation won't get tarnished?"

His face reddened and to Lace, that was as good as an admission of guilt. She started to stand and he grabbed her. "Wait a minute. It's not like that at all. I've always tried to be discreet, something readily agreed on by the ladies involved, and this was the easiest way. But I haven't been there since I first met you and I only ask now so that we can be alone together, uninterrupted."

"You don't want anyone to know we're sleeping together!"

He pulled off his glasses and rubbed his face. "Lace, I'm not ashamed of being with you, if that's what you think. But I think we need time alone together to sort things out."

"What's there to sort? We wanted each other. It's as simple as that."

"Nothing about it was simple and you know it."

"It was for me."

He shook his head. "Okay, then. You say you slept with me because you wanted to. So what's changed? And don't tell me you don't want me anymore, because I won't believe you."

She didn't have a ready answer. And despite her arguments and indignation, she desperately wanted to go with him. "I'll have to think about it."

He made a sound of disgust and stood. "You do that."

Lace watched him begin snatching up tattered paper from the floor with excess energy. He wadded it into tight balls and hurled it all into the fireplace, where the paper burst into colorful flames. Lace stood to help him, her thoughts whirling.

As she tossed her own wad of paper into the fire, Lace shook her head. Daniel would someday get over his ridiculous conclusions that love was harmful and too powerful. Then he'd marry some prim and proper little lady, probably a doctor's daughter or some such, and he'd live happily ever after in esteemed propriety.

And, like her mother, she'd miss him forever.

Lace squeezed her eyes shut and tried to push that troubling thought away, but it had rooted itself deeply and she felt buried beneath it. A wad of paper hit her in the rump and she turned. Max grinned at her.

"Sorry. You're blocking the fireplace."

With an evil smile and a sigh of relief to be distracted, Lace wadded another ball. Max went running. He caught Guy, who'd just started to wander in, and used him as a shield. Unfortunately, Lace had already let the wadded paper ball fly and it hit Guy square in the chest. He went stock-still and stared.

Lace took a step back, trying to stifle her laughter, but the expression on Guy's face proved to be too much and she giggled.

"Okay, then." Guy advanced, slowly, keeping Lace in his sights. Lace held out her hands, trying to ward him off even as she laughed some more. Just as he was ready to pounce, Annie slipped up behind him and slapped a huge red bow to the top of his head, where it clung to his short hair. Guy whirled on her and they both went running. Max watched them go, then hustled around the room gathering up new paper bombs, preparing for their return. He loaded up his arms and crept off after them.

Daniel slipped his arm around Lace. "They're all nuts, aren't they?"

She smiled. "Wonderfully so. You don't mind that they're racing through your house?"

"Why should I?"

Since she couldn't think of a single reason, she shrugged. They heard squealing from the guest bedroom and Max came tearing out, Guy right behind him, pelting him repeatedly in the back of the head with the paper bombs. They flashed past into the kitchen where a loud crash followed. Annie, her feet now missing her sexy high-heeled shoes, came through with her own arsenal, in hot pursuit.

"While we have a moment alone, tell me you'll go to the cabin with me." He tipped up her face, kissed her lightly and whispered, "I need you, Lace."

Her lungs squeezed tight and her heart expanded. There was really no reason to fight it, she decided, gladly giving up her resistance. "Yes, I'll go with you."

His eyes turned hot and she felt it clear to the bottom of her stomach. "You won't regret it, Lace. I promise."

Oh, that tone of voice, the meaning behind the words. She leaned toward him, and Max shouted, "We're going outside to build a snowman. Want to come along?"

Guilty, they jumped apart. When Lace looked at Max, he didn't taunt her. He kept his brows raised in a mildly curious expression.

"Mmm, how about I help Daniel clean up, then I'll make some hot chocolate for when you come back in?"

Max shrugged. "If you're sure you won't join us?" His gaze traveled from Lace to Daniel and back again. They both shook their heads.

He narrowed his gaze. "All right, then. But you two behave yourselves in here. Don't do anything I wouldn't do."

Laughing, Lace pointed a finger at him. "There isn't anything you wouldn't do!"

"Oh, yeah. In that case, have at it." He gave Daniel a salute and seconds later he and Guy trudged outside.

Annie ran past to the guest bedroom, and when she reappeared she wore jeans as tattered as Guy's, with scuffed boots, one of Daniel's old sweatshirts and his coat. She waved on her way out.

"My sister, the tomboy. What a relief. For a minute

there, when she showed up in that damn killer dress, I thought I'd lost her forever.''

Lace took in the affectionate smile on his face and felt compelled to warn him. ''You'll never lose her, Daniel, but the woman in the red dress is as much a part of Annie now as the tomboy. Just as you've saved her old clothes, you now have to accept the new. And even you have to admit she looked terrific.''

Instead of admitting anything, Daniel looped his arms around her and kissed her long and deep. His hands cupped her bottom and he urged her closer. ''What I noticed is how good you look.'' He stared at her mouth, speaking through small nipping kisses. ''You're beautiful.''

Embarrassed, she pulled away and forced a laugh. ''I imagine I look wrecked after crying and making a fool of myself.''

''No one thought you were a fool, least of all me.'' He studied her face. ''Tell me how you've been this past week. You didn't overdo it, did you?''

''With my friendly neighbors dropping in to help, not to mention Annie and Max? No, I didn't overdo.''

Daniel stepped closer, looming over her. She knew that look, the one he employed when irritated, and she braced herself. ''Your neighbor? The guy with all the gold chains and the killer dog?''

''The dog is being trained and already shows much better manners. The neighbor is full of gratitude because I was so understanding. He offered to pick up my mail and paper since you weren't there to intimidate him.'' She lifted her chin. ''I declined his offer.''

Daniel relaxed and she rolled her eyes. ''For heaven's sake, you couldn't really be worried about him.''

''Not worried. I just don't like him.''

"Why?"

He muttered something, then threw out his arms in exasperation. "His damn dog tried to have you for breakfast. That's reason enough, isn't it? Now tell me when we can leave."

Wondering if Guy had been right, if Daniel could possibly be jealous, she decided to let it drop. "Instead, why don't I give you your present?"

His brows lifted. "I wait with bated breath."

Lace went to a bag she'd set in the entry hall and carried it back to where Daniel stood by the tree. He hadn't moved. She handed him the first gift from the bag. He turned it this way and that, shook it, squeezed it.

"Oh, for heaven's sake, will you just open it?"

"All right." He tore the package open and removed a pair of lemon yellow silk briefs. Lace bit her lip to hold back the laughter while Daniel examined his gift from every possible angle. Finally he said, "The color will do wonders for my eyes."

Lace coughed, which turned into a snicker, and finally a robust laugh. When she started to quiet, she took one look at Daniel, and lost it again.

"Brat."

"I'm sorry." She took deep breaths to gain control. "Does this mean you don't like your gift?"

"I like it fine, as long as you don't expect me to wear it."

"Oh, but I do." She bobbed her eyebrows as she said it. "I can already picture it."

"Well, don't."

"I have one more thing for you."

"More underwear?"

She chuckled again, but shook her head. "No. Something else."

This package was smaller and she warned him not to shake it.

It was wrapped in a way that the lid came off without tearing the gold foil paper and Daniel treated it gently, setting the lid aside. He pushed back the tissue paper and then stared. "A pocket watch."

Lace licked her lips, overcome with nervousness. "Annie told me you didn't wear a wristwatch because it bothered you. I thought this way you could drop it into your pocket."

He lifted the watch out carefully, as if it were made of fine crystal. Lace practically bounced beside him, hoping he'd like it, afraid he wouldn't. He studied the watch, hefted it in his palm.

Lace swallowed, then summoned every ounce of her courage. "I had it engraved on the back."

His gaze flicked to her face and then back to the watch. He turned it over in his palm and read the inscription. "Dr. Daniel Sawyers—brother, friend, physician." His eyes met hers. "I don't understand."

It was impossible to stay still, and she shifted again. "That's what you are," she explained with a small shrug. "All those things. You understand what it means to be family, to have responsibilities. And you take those responsibilities to Max and Annie very seriously. And you're the very best doctor I've ever known and an incredibly good friend to Guy. I didn't know how to say it…how to put into words how much I admire you for that."

He touched her cheek and she rambled even more. "I know we argue a lot and I sometimes insult you."

"Sometimes."

"So I wanted you to know how I really feel, that I'm glad to know you and that I think you're an incredibly good man."

He stepped close, crowding her, the watch now gripped in his fist. He wouldn't let her look away, wouldn't let her hide from the admission of her words.

"Do…do you like it okay?"

"I like the watch very much. I like the inscription even better." He kissed her, and there was so much in that kiss, things she couldn't begin to comprehend, but she felt them all the same.

She blinked up at him and he smiled. "Thank you, Lace."

"Well." Lace felt at a loss for further words. The way he watched her made her feel vulnerable and she didn't like it. With a false laugh, she stepped away and clasped her hands together. "I'm glad this is working out. Maybe this little trip you have planned to the cabin will clear the air, get rid of some of the sexual tension between us, and we'll actually be able to be friends instead of adversaries. What do you think, Daniel?"

When she looked up, Daniel again looked remote. He turned the watch over in his palm, shook his head and stuck it in his pocket. "With you, Lace, I never know what the hell to expect. I think I'll just wait and be surprised."

Nine

Daniel watched her walk around, pretending to familiarize herself with the cabin. She looked ready to jump out of her skin. He smiled to himself and slipped up behind her. "Are you nervous?"

She jerked, then turned to face him. "Nervous? No. Why would I be nervous, for heaven's sake?"

Her gaze darted around, studying every inch of the cabin. She looked at the fireplace, where he'd already started a fire, and then to the candles he'd lit to provide added muted light, to help set the mood.

Looping his arms around her, he anchored her to him and nuzzled her neck. "Maybe you're nervous because you're not as worldly as you like to pretend. Because being with a man, and making love, is new to you."

"Ha!" She pushed against his chest, putting space between them. "We've already done…" She waved at the bed. "This."

"Not really." Daniel slipped her cape off her shoulders and draped it over a chair. If she had any inkling of the things he wanted to do to her, that he planned to do to her, he had no doubt she'd be twice as skittish.

The cabin was small, with a king-size bed in the only bedroom, visible through the open door. A plush furniture grouping sat to one side of the living room, forming a conversation pit that faced a large stone fireplace. A state-of-the-art entertainment center occupied one entire wall. Scented candles were situated everywhere, even, she had noted, in the bathroom, which was equipped with a Jacuzzi tub.

The cabin was a place of seduction, a retreat meant to indulge the senses. It was obvious he intended to indulge Lace very thoroughly. And himself in the bargain.

"Lace, it's okay to be a little unsure of yourself. Talking about sex and making love are two different things."

She stiffened and turned to glare at him. "Are you suggesting I don't know what I'm talking about?"

At the moment every word she said, every action, delighted him. She was so womanly, and she was his. No man had been with her except him, and she was here with him now. He felt exuberant, alive and nothing could damage his mood.

"Sweetheart, I'm only suggesting that you might be a little unsure of yourself. After all, despite all your vocalizing on the subject, you have very little hands-on practice."

"That doesn't mean I don't understand—"

Daniel kissed her. He didn't want to waste another single second debating the issue. Finesse was the last thing on his mind, and he kissed her with all the hunger, greed and urgency he felt. He pushed his tongue into her mouth, then groaned when she touched her own to his.

"Damn, Lace…"

He kissed her again. She cuddled close, pressing her body into his, trying to get closer. Their clothes were in the way and he wanted her naked, now, but he pulled back. She went on tiptoe to try to kiss him again, and he had to hold her back.

"Just a minute, Lace. Let me catch my breath."

"Why?"

He hugged her tight, charmed by her innocence. "Lace, what we did the last time, that wasn't even close to what it should be. I goofed, mostly because I wanted you too much and I rushed things."

"It felt right to me."

"Which only goes to show that what I said is true. You need more experience. With me."

She looked around the cabin again and scowled. "It certainly seems you've had enough practice. I can't believe you have this place, that you sneak here for your little rendezvous."

"I don't sneak, I'm only discreet. How many times do I have to tell you that?"

"Who else knows about this place?"

He sighed. When Lace wanted a fight, she was like a bulldog with a meaty bone. "My father knows. And Guy and Max."

With her hands on her slim hips and the most evil expression he'd ever seen in her eyes, she stalked up to him until they were nose to nose. "I see. All the men know. But not poor little innocent Annie."

"There's no reason for Annie to know…"

"Have Guy and Max used this place?"

He felt like squirming, but resisted the inclination. "It's not my place to say what other men have…"

"Ha! In other words, they have. So this is the 'guys'

place,' is that it? This is where the men hang out when they want to do lascivious things?''

With his teeth gnashing together, Daniel agreed. ''It allots a certain amount of privacy, yes.''

''So. What if Annie had wanted to indulge in some lascivious pursuits? You prefer she does her rendez-vousing out in the open? You would keep this palace of private seduction from her?''

He removed his glasses and rubbed his eyes. ''All right. I'm a male chauvinist pig. Feel better? I wallow in the double standard and I probably always will, at least where my little sister is concerned.'' He sighed and gave her a questioning look. ''How the hell did I go from apologizing for my feeble performance to discussing my lack of understanding on the feminine sexual revolution?''

She grinned at him and shrugged. ''I'm sorry. But it just rankles that you have this place.''

''Why? I thought you believed in mature, adult rela-tionships. You know how I feel…*felt,* about getting in-volved.'' Lace didn't notice his correction, and Daniel decided not to rush his fences. Especially with her being so prickly. ''I'm a man, Lace. I have the same urges as any other.''

''Not toward me, you didn't. At least, not until you found out I was a virgin. Now I'm suddenly good enough to grace your little cabin?''

Okay, so my good humor isn't endless. Daniel twisted his jaw, trying to hold the words back, but Lace tapped her foot on the hardwood floor and he lost the struggle.

''Dammit, can I help how I feel, Lace? I can't deny that I'm…flattered to be the only man you've been with. But I swear, if you hadn't been a virgin, I'd still have asked you here. Long before we made love, I knew I was fighting a losing battle. And I might be a fraud, but I'm not a total hypocrite. I don't expect all women to be virginal.''

Lace plopped down on the couch and put her hands on her knees. ''I suppose I can understand. Most people do tend to feel territorial in these situations.''

He bit his upper lip, not overly thrilled with his feelings being termed a *situation*. She started to articulate on her latest theory, but Daniel held up his hands. ''I concede to your professional assessment. In fact,'' he lied with a convincing air, determined to get things back on his designated track, ''I was hoping you'd give me a demonstration of all your assembled knowledge.''

She didn't look insulted by his suggestion. She looked intrigued.

He held out his arms like a sacrifice. ''I'm waiting to benefit from your wealth of scientific edification.''

''Is that so?'' She pushed herself up from the couch and came to stand in front of him. He dropped his arms and smiled. ''Anxious to get started, are you?''

He traced her collarbone with one finger and watched her shiver. ''Very anxious. Will you enlighten me with your accumulated wisdom? Will you instruct me?''

She bit her lip, then looked at him suspiciously. He saw comprehension in her gaze, and then stubborn determination. She blushed, but she stared him in the eye. His groin tightened when he realized what that look meant.

''Certainly, Daniel. I'll instruct you. If you're sure you want me to.''

His lungs constricted, but he managed to croak, ''Absolutely.'' Hell, he'd had fantasies about it. ''You just tell me what to do, and I'll do it.''

She nodded, resolute. ''Okay. First off, I think you're

right. We rushed things the last time. Not that it wasn't wonderful, but…we should try to get to know each other's preferences a little more.''

He preferred her naked, moaning his name while he watched her climax, but he kept the thought to himself.

''Fine. What would you like to know?''

''Let's get comfortable, shall we?''

She took his hand and led him to the couch in front of the fireplace. He sat and she half sprawled beside him, her long legs stretched out, her arm on the couch behind him. She toyed with his shirt collar, her breasts pressed into his shoulder. The witch.

''Now, Daniel, tell me what turns you on.''

He swallowed. All right, if she wanted to play games, he could hold his own. ''You turn me on.''

''No, no, no. More specific. What is it a woman does that you like?''

His gaze narrowed and he considered his replies. She was right when she said he'd been more conventional in his activities. He'd certainly never spoken so openly about his preferences with a woman. But with Lace, he felt challenged.

''I like it when a woman isn't restrained. When she moans to let me know how she feels—the way you did.''

Lace blushed. He smiled and expounded on his confession. ''You moan very nicely, honey. Deep and raw and real.''

She cleared her throat and slipped her hand inside his shirt. ''Anything else?''

''Yes. The way you moved. I touched you and you pushed against my fingers, my mouth.'' He was hard, aching. His blood rushed through his veins. ''And I like the way you smell. All soft and female and sweet.''

''Daniel…''

He cupped her breast and found her nipple stiff and beckoning. He toyed with it and Lace closed her eyes, a soft moan escaping her lips. "Just like that, Lace. You like it when I touch you here, don't you?"

She pierced him with a look so intent, so hot, he almost gasped. "I like it better when it's your mouth."

He stripped her shirt over her head and tugged down her bra. At the last second he caught himself. He licked her, letting his tongue flick and hearing her small anxious breaths.

Without hesitation, she said, "I want you to suck me, Daniel."

His control shot to hell, he did as she asked, moaning with her as he drew her into the heat of his mouth. He left her nipple wet and blew on it, his breath causing it to pucker even more. Then he switched to her other breast.

Lace reached for his shirt and began tugging it off, her movements no longer calculated, but frenzied. "Don't you want to hear all the things I like, Daniel?"

"Absolutely," he mumbled while helping her remove his shirt, at the same time continuing to kiss her soft flesh.

"I like your chest." She pulled away enough to run her fingers through the hair there. "When I first saw you sleeping at my apartment and I saw your chest, it made me feel funny."

"Funny how?" His voice was breathless, almost as breathless as hers.

"All tingly and warm. I'd never really wanted anyone before, I don't think." She shook her head. "No, that's a lie. I'd wanted you before that, too. Just not quite that badly."

"You should have told me."

"Mmm." She let her fingers trail down to his slacks. "I should have had my wicked way with you, knowing what you think of me?"

He kicked off his shoes as she tackled his belt. "I don't think you're wicked."

She chuckled. "I know. Now you mistakenly think I'm some innocent little maid." She licked his chin, and then his chest. "But I am wicked. Very wicked."

"I never said…"

"Take off your clothes, Daniel, and let's go to bed."

He shouldn't have been surprised. Lace was out to prove a point, and he knew, whatever the point might be, he'd enjoy it. He grinned, daring her with a look. "I will if you will."

A smile twitched on her mouth, then she stood and very casually stripped in front of him. He could barely breathe; every muscle in his body turned rock-hard. As she removed each article of clothing, she watched him— and lectured.

"A lot of women are terribly shy about being naked. Did you know that, Daniel?"

He nodded dumbly, his mouth dry at the sight of her.

"They think their bodies are inferior because they try to compare themselves to all the nude models in men's magazines. It's hard to convince them that men don't expect perfection, that no two bodies are alike and that's a good thing. Breasts are different, different sizes, shapes. Nipples can be pink or mauve or—"

"Lace."

"Some men like petite women, but a lot of them like a woman with a few extra pounds."

He leaned forward and kissed her belly, his hands going to her bottom, cuddling her, touching her. She tangled her fingers in his hair and he said, "Your body is perfect."

She laughed. "I'm far from perfect, but I'm glad you approve, because I'm not ashamed of my body."

Slipping his hands into her panties, he felt the softness of her bottom, her plump flesh, before skimming them down her legs. She stepped out of them and moved back. "Your turn, Daniel."

He stood and undid his slacks. When he started to push them down his hips, Lace knelt in front of him and took over the task. He locked his knees to remain standing.

"Do you know what you're doing to me?" She'd positioned herself as a sexual supplicant, and his male brain became frantic at the sight.

"Of course I do." She peeked up at him. "And I know what I'm *going* to do to you."

He groaned, causing her to laugh. "I haven't done it yet, Daniel."

"It doesn't matter." He trembled like a virgin himself when she wrapped her small hands around his hardened arousal. He squeezed his eyes shut and clenched his jaw. "My imagination is going wild here, Lace."

"In all my studies, there was one particular thing that intrigued me, that stirred my curiosity."

"Lace…"

"Do you know what that one thing is, Daniel?"

He groaned.

"I suppose I should just show you."

The warning given, she leaned forward and he felt her mouth close around him. He yelled, and Lace paused. "I've never done this, but I like it. Are you okay? Am I doing this wrong?" She stroked him lightly, then replaced her fingers with her tongue. "Or this?"

He couldn't get air into his constricted lungs, so he couldn't very well talk. He shook his head.

"You'll tell me if you want me to do something different?"

He nodded, and his hand tangled in her hair, urging her back to her seduction.

It was the most exquisite, most sensually exciting thing a woman had ever done with him. And since it certainly wasn't his first time, he decided it had to be Lace. She was different from every other woman he knew, so being with her, making love with her, was different. Not just unique, but better, more intense, thrilling.

When he knew he couldn't take it anymore, he pulled away. She looked dazed and warm and very aroused. Her breasts, flushed with excitement, rose and fell with her rapid breathing. The fact that what she'd been doing had excited her, too, made him full with emotion.

He scooped her up into his arms and carried her to the bed. "It's my turn, sweetheart," he said between warm, gentling kisses. He felt ready to burst with some vague, heavy sense of perfection and he couldn't quit touching her, kissing her.

Lace wound her arms around his neck. "That was your turn."

"No. My turn is getting to watch you as you climax."

Her lashes lowered over her eyes. "Daniel."

He smiled at her pink cheeks and laid her carefully in the middle of the bed. "You like it." Keeping his gaze on her, he opened the closet and located a box of condoms. He set them on the nightstand. "You like the way I talk to you. It excites you."

Lace widened her eyes at the box, then admitted, "Actually, it does. But then, everything about you excites me."

His heart skipped a beat. "Is that a fact?" He stretched out beside her. "I could just look at you and be happy."

"But I might not like it."

Her muscles tightened when he laid a hand on her belly. "Do you like this?"

"Hmm." Her lips parted.

"And this?"

"Daniel…" She breathed his name.

His hand slid between her thighs, light and teasing. He stroked. "Do you know what I'm going to do to you, Lace?"

With her eyes closed and her body taut, she whispered, "What?"

He leaned over and whispered in her ear, and she moaned, pressing her head back, offering herself to him. He kissed her breasts and her belly and when he moved between her thighs she groaned in heightened anticipation of his promise.

Daniel loved every sound she made, every movement. She was so open, so free and honest and *real*. He kissed her deeply, heady with the taste and scent of her body. He brought her to an explosive climax, loving the way she screamed and clutched at him and praised him. And before the small convulsions had ended, he thrust into her. Once again, she shuddered and cried out his name, this time taking him with her as she came, and beyond his release, he realized something else.

He loved Lace McGee.

Lace was the most uninhibited lover he'd ever known, ever imagined. She had no modesty once she got used to being nude with him. In fact, in the four days they'd been at the cabin, they'd seldom bothered with clothes, and she'd quit blushing after the first day.

She was also the most talented, demanding lover he'd ever known. Lace could make him lose his control with just a look. When she talked sexy to him, he went wild. And when she touched him, quickly learning through her openness and honesty what pleased him most, he couldn't hold back.

Lace was a very quick learner.

Daniel thought it could take him a lifetime to get used to her. Only he didn't have a lifetime. Lace would only grant him a short interlude of intimacy. She'd been very specific that their affair had a limited time period. He could understand her reasoning. They were from different worlds. His, staid and conservative and stifling. Lace would smother in his extended company, and he'd sooner give her up than ever make her unhappy.

She slept beside him on her stomach and he admired the smooth line of her back and rounded bottom. She'd healed nicely, he noticed with a professional eye, her scar only a thin pink line. In another month, it would barely be noticeable. He traced it with his fingertip and she stretched awake.

Turning her head on the pillow to look at him, she smiled. "Good morning."

He continued touching special places on her body, lightly, teasingly. Behind her knees, the small of her back. Down the length of her spine and beyond.

"Mmm-hmm." She purred, smiling. "I like that."

Without meaning to, he asked, "Do you like me?"

She rolled onto her back and faced him, her green eyes slumberous, her pale hair spread out on the pillow. "I think you're the finest of men."

"Lace." Lying back down beside her, he propped his

head on a fist and made a big production of stroking her belly. "I'm being serious."

"Of course I like you. Do you think I'd sleep with a man I didn't like?" When he didn't answer, she sighed and sat up, cross-legged, unselfconscious in her nudity. "Daniel, just because we're so different doesn't mean I can't understand who you are. I've always been free to do as I please, responsible only for myself. But you, you've always been out to save the world."

He smiled, though he felt unreasonably sad. "Not the whole world. Just my small part of it."

She smoothed his hair. "Have I ever told you how sexy I think your glasses are?"

Laughing, he wondered how she could come up with such inane things to say at the most improbable times.

"You look so intellectual, so serious and professional."

"You look like a vamp, sitting there like that, seducing me. And here I was hoping to have a serious, professional conversation."

Lace pulled a pillow in front of her. It barely covered the high points of interest. "There. Behold a modest woman."

Unable to resist a moment more, he kissed her, but they both ended up laughing. That was another thing he loved about Lace. She could make everything fun. She lightened his life with her teasing insults and her absurd taunts. She'd forced him to drop his cloak of propriety, and he'd honestly enjoyed every moment.

He'd also learned to trust her instincts.

"You don't have a modest bone in your body, but I've decided you are very astute when it comes to my sister."

She stilled, all teasing gone. "Is that so?"

"Yes. I thought about it, and I watched her. You're right, she is in love. I'm not sure who it is, and—" he looked at her over the rim of his glasses "—don't suppose you'll tell me?"

Lace shook her head. "I can't. I promised."

He accepted that. Lace would never break a promise, and he wouldn't ask her to. "The problem is, I'm afraid she's going to get hurt."

Lace took a deep breath. "I'm afraid of the same thing. I've tried to warn her, to…"

"To tell her love doesn't exist?"

She looked away. "No. That's not my place to say. I've never tried to discourage people from seeking love. But I want Annie to be prepared. Even the examples of supposed love I've seen have been unrewarding, unhappy experiences most of the time. People end up hurt. Annie's so free with herself. She doesn't know to protect her heart."

He wondered if that's what Lace was doing: protecting her heart. But he seriously doubted her heart was involved with him. She'd made it clear, way too many times, how different they both were. He remembered her accusing him of hiding, and knew it to be true. Even now, he hid, because the truth would be too bitter, too painful, to deal with.

"You've been a good friend to her, Lace. She should have been able to come to me, but I was too busy trying to force her to stay the same. I see that now."

Lace put her arms around him. "Be happy for her, Daniel, even if things don't work out. She's a wonderful person, a beautiful, caring woman, and you're the reason why. You've done an incredible job with her."

"You give me too much credit," he said, but he liked hearing it. He liked knowing there were things about him that Lace admired. He took her shielding pillow and tossed it across the floor, then pulled her naked body against his own as he fell back on the bed. ''Make love to me, Lace.''

She cupped his face and kissed him while she straddled his hips. He raised his palms to her breasts and watched her head fall back, her eyes close.

Someday Lace would find a man as forthright and uninhibited as herself. Then she'd give up her ridiculous notions that love didn't exist and she'd marry him, living her life independently of society's strictures. Being free in a way he never could be.

The thought filled him with rage and remorse, but he tamped it down. He didn't want her love, didn't want to tie himself to a woman the way his father had. As Lace had pointed out, a lot of people depended on him and he couldn't let them down, couldn't take chances with their happiness.

Which meant he couldn't take a chance with Lace.

She didn't believe in love, and that made her the worst possible risk. And although she claimed to like him, liking wouldn't be enough, not between them. He and Lace had no future together, and he'd known it from the start.

All he could do was take the time he had with her, and then let her go.

He caught Lace and pulled her beneath him. She blinked up at him in surprise. ''I thought you wanted me to make love to you?''

''I changed my mind. I want us to make love to each other.'' He stared at her, trying to find something he knew didn't exist. Lace closed her eyes against his probing gaze.

He cupped her jaw, almost roughly, regaining her attention. He saw confusion and distress, and he couldn't bear it. He kissed her hard, his tongue thrusting, his mouth eating at hers, devouring, and for a long time, he couldn't stop kissing her. When he finally did, they were both numb with pleasure.

Later that day his beeper signaled the end to their idyll.

Ten

January was a miserable month of sleet and cold. It seemed he'd no sooner stopped seeing Lace than the sun stopped shining and winter lost its appeal.

Everyone appeared to be in the doldrums, his family included. They'd been hanging around lately, watching football games or playing cards and generally making nuisances of themselves, Guy especially.

"I've had it. I'm going to head home." Guy, sitting on the opposite end of the sofa and eating popcorn, yawned hugely.

Daniel pulled out his pocket watch, fingered the engraving on the back as he always did, and checked the time. "It's only ten o'clock. What's your rush?"

"You. You're miserable company."

As much as he wanted to deny it, he knew it was true. "Like you're so choosy?" Daniel flicked off the sports channel they'd both been ignoring and tossed the remote on the table.

"I know when to get away from a bear."

Max, doing sit-ups on the floor at their feet, grunted a muffled, "Amen," to Guy's comment.

Daniel nudged him in the ribs with the toe of his shoe. "Not a word out of you."

Guy stared at Max. "What's with him, anyway? Why all the exercise all of a sudden?"

Daniel shrugged. His brother's peculiarities always eluded him. "You planning on entering a body-building contest, Max?"

"Nope." He huffed between counting. "Ninety-nine, one hundred." He fell back on the floor, breathing deeply. After a minute he pushed himself to a sitting position. "Just staying in shape. I was thinking of taking another trip."

"Where to this time?" Daniel hated it when Max traveled, but his brother had a bad case of wanderlust and there was no curtailing his interest. He wondered what Lace would say about Max's tendency to run off for long stretches.

He no sooner thought it than he shook his head. He and Lace were history, and unlike his father, he was determined not to mope.

"What?" Max stared at his brother in confusion. "You're shaking your head at me and frowning and I haven't even said anything yet."

Guy laughed. "He was probably thinking of a certain blonde bombshell who shall remain nameless."

"Who? Lace?"

Guy tossed a pillow at Max. "Don't throttle him, Dan. Lace is the only blond bombshell we know at present."

Max snorted. "Not me. I could name a dozen."

Daniel held up his hands. "Enough, all right?"

Guy stood, then stepped over Max. "It's not enough. You miss her. Hell, we all do, except Annie. She still sees her." He pointed a finger at Daniel. "Your little sister has been especially weird lately. You should keep an eye on her."

Daniel waved away his concern. "Be patient with her. She's in love."

Both Guy and Max gawked at him. "What!"

"You guys should pay better attention." Daniel didn't add that it had taken Lace's prodding for him to notice and be convinced.

Guy slowly sat back in his seat. "She's in love? With who?"

"Hell if I know. I wish I did because the jerk is making her unhappy."

Guy stared at him. "She won't tell you?"

"No." Then Daniel looked struck. "You should talk to her, Guy. She feels funny talking to me because I'm her brother and she's afraid I'll disapprove."

Max stood and put his hands on his hips. "If the guy is making her sad, then you can bet I disapprove! I'll find out who he is and—"

"No, don't interfere, Max. Annie's all grown up and she has to handle things on her own."

Guy shook his head. "I'll talk to her." He looked galvanized with new purpose. "I'll stop by and talk to her tonight."

Daniel stared at him. "Uh, Guy, not a good idea. It's getting late and you know Annie has to be up early to open the bookstore. Just stop in and see her tomorrow at work."

"Right. Tomorrow. I'll do that." Guy stuck his hat

on his head, picked up his coat and walked out without another word.

Max chortled. "I think you're both pathetic." Then to Daniel, "Why don't you just call Lace? Tell her how you feel?"

For the first time that he could really remember, Daniel wanted to talk to his brother about his problems. He didn't want to burden him, but he needed his advice, and Max knew more about women than most three men put together.

He looked at Max and said, "I wish I could, but I'm afraid to."

Max blinked at the outpouring of brotherly confidence, started to say something, changed his mind and pulled up a chair. "What do you mean, you're afraid? You don't think she'll be glad to hear from you?"

"I have no idea. You probably don't know this, but—"

"You and Lace were involved? Of course I knew it. I probably knew before you did that you were hung up on her. That's why I chased her in front of you."

"To annoy me?"

"To get you going before she got away." Max gave him a wide grin and Daniel laughed. "She cares about you, too."

Daniel's smile froze. "You can tell?"

"Lace is a very open person. She's easy to read."

"Damn." Daniel slumped back in his seat and rubbed the back of his neck. "The thing is, she likes me okay, I think. And we're…compatible in some ways."

Max gave a sage nod of understanding. "Uh-huh."

"But I don't know if she loves me. And if she doesn't, and I pursue this, I could end up like Dad."

Max whistled. ''You really have been stewing on this, haven't you?''

''I don't ever want to be like that. I don't ever want to forget the people around me and end up living in a void.''

Max let his hands dangle between his spread knees and considered things. After a moment he looked up and stared at Daniel. ''I hate to be overly blunt, but you're being an idiot.''

''Gee, I'm glad you decided to soften that for me.''

''You're nothing like our father, Daniel. He's flighty and irresponsible and even though we know he cares, he's not the type of person you could ever depend on.''

Though he tried to hide it, Daniel was shocked. Max had seldom mentioned their father's vagaries, and never with such vehemence. But now Daniel realized just how much Max had observed. Trying to make excuses for their father, Daniel said, ''He misses Mom.''

''Bull. I'll bet he was that way his entire life. Just as you've been a rock for as long as I can remember. I've always known you were there for me. So has Annie. I don't for a second believe you'd ever forget either of us, so don't use that lame excuse as a reason not to call Lace.''

''But…''

Max waved him to silence. ''You're miserable now, but you haven't abandoned anyone. And you never will.''

Put that way, it did seem pretty absurd. Daniel couldn't really imagine not caring about his brother or sister, even Guy and his father. Or Lace.

''Give it up, Dan. You're as rock-solid stable as they come and nothing and no one is going to change that.''

''That could be a problem, too, you know. I mean,

Lace is so different from me. She probably finds me boring.''

Max puffed up his chest like an affronted turkey. ''If you've bored her, then you're an insult to the Sawyers machismo and I'm disowning you as a brother.''

''I don't mean I…'' Daniel floundered, then shook his head. ''What I mean is, we're very different people.''

''Opposites attract. Not a problem.''

Daniel chewed that over, and then shook his head. ''I don't know.''

''Look at it this way. If you're miserable—and believe me, you are—imagine how Lace must feel. You haven't called her in a damned month.''

Daniel felt a pain in his heart at the thought of Lace being unhappy. ''Why do you think she's been miserable?''

''Because I for one listen to her show. And I've been by to see her. She and Annie have taken to crying in their colas together at that same bar where Annie got picked up by the police. Which by the way, wasn't Lace's fault.''

''I know. It was just another example of Annie's stubbornness.''

''There are a lot of men at those bars.''

Daniel halted his dejected study of his shoes and shot Max a glare. ''Your point being?''

''Lace is a very sexy woman. She gets hit on all the time. She and Annie both do.''

Anger propelled him from his seat and carried him to within an inch of Max. ''And you just sit there and allow it, I suppose?''

''Nope. That's why I've been hanging out there with them. So I can scare off all the prospects. Though I doubt it was necessary. Not once has Lace or Annie acted interested in anyone.''

That was something at least. ''Oh, hell, what radio station is she on?''

Max laughed the entire time he tuned in the station for Daniel, then he bowed. ''I have to go. I'll let you sit here and suffer alone awhile. It'll be good for your character.''

Max was just through the door when Daniel shook himself out of his stupor and jogged after him. ''Max, wait.''

''What?''

''You said you're thinking of taking another trip.''

''So?''

Daniel crossed his arms over his chest, trying to block some of the cold. ''You're not leaving anytime soon, are you?''

Max looked wary. ''I don't know. Why?''

With a weary sigh and a smile, Daniel slapped him on the shoulder. ''Last time you left without telling me. This time I'd like to know first. And if it's at all possible, I'd like you to hang around for a little while longer. I might need more advice.''

Max studied him, uncertainty written on his face, then he nodded. ''All right. Sure.'' He started to turn away, and then added, ''If I decide to go, I'll let you know beforehand.''

''I appreciate it. And Max?''

''Yeah?''

''Thanks. For everything.''

Again Max studied him, then nodded. Seconds later he disappeared down the walk.

Daniel went back into the house, rubbing his arms to warm himself after being outside, clapping his hands

against his body. It was damned cold out, but colder still
inside himself. He'd done Lace a terrible wrong, treated
her abominably, worse than he'd ever considered himself
capable of treating a woman.

He loved her, missed her. He wanted to make love to
her right now, this very minute, to talk with her and
discuss his family and all their foibles. He wanted to
argue with her until he was blue in the face and until
she lost her temper and then he'd make love to her some
more and let her wear him out. He'd convince her—
somehow—that all her reasoning on love, and his reasoning, as well, was pure nonsense. They were intelligent people, even though his intelligence hadn't been
much in evidence of late. They would....

His ears suddenly prickled with the sound of Lace
speaking on the radio. Damn, he'd been so busy allowing his mind to meander, ruminating on all the ways he
intended to fix things between them, he'd missed a good
portion of her show. He pulled up a chair and permitted
himself to be soothed by her gentle, concerned tone.

"You can't sit back and wait for things to right themselves on their own, Ally. If you love him, you have to
take charge of the situation and tell him."

The woman, a young woman judging by the sound of
things, spoke uncertainly. "I'm not sure how he feels,
and now he says he's being transferred and he didn't
exactly ask me to come with him…"

"So?" Lace's voice, so sweet and sure and caring,
stroked over Daniel, warming him from the inside out.
A gnawing ache started in his gut and swelled until he
wanted to howl. He wanted to be with her, right this
instant, but she continued talking, and he continued to
listen.

"Love is always worth taking a chance on. And that

means honesty, from both of you. It's a myth that men are always confident and brazen. Perhaps he loves you, but he's feeling as vulnerable and unsure of the entire situation as you are. You'll never know unless you ask. And isn't it worth the risk of a little heartache, a modicum of embarrassment, to find out? If you just let him leave, you'll never know, and surely that will hurt worse than the truth, whatever the truth might be.''

The girl's voice quavered, then finally she said, ''You're right. He did…did look at me funny, kind of watchful, when he told me he'd been transferred. Maybe he was waiting for me to say something.''

''Maybe he was waiting for a declaration of your feelings.'' Lace's tone gentled, became thoughtful, when she continued. ''There's no guarantees in life. It's so easy to find love and lose it, to mistake love for the wrong emotions. Trying to guard your heart could cause you to lose the one you want. And any good relationship, any lasting relationship, should begin with total honesty. Tell him how you feel, then demand that he do the same.''

With new resolution, the woman said, ''I will! Right now. And thank you. Thank you for everything.''

Daniel could hear the smile in Lace's voice, in her words. ''Thank you, Ally. I hope things work out, but if they don't and you want to talk, you know how to reach me.''

''I do. But you're right about one thing. Knowing will be better than not knowing. If he doesn't care, I'll handle it, but at least I'll be certain I didn't throw anything important away.''

''You know, Ally, you're a very smart young woman. I have a feeling you'll be just fine.''

Both women laughed softly, and then the radio station broke for a commercial. Daniel surged to his feet, innervated with new purpose. He'd heard enough, more than enough. Damn her, how could she say all those things and not believe in love! It was past time the woman began to heed her own words, and he intended to insist that she start right now. He grabbed up his coat, not his warmest but the closest to hand, and went through the house to the garage. If he hurried, he'd catch her at the station. He shivered with the cold as he pulled out of the driveway, then smiled with anticipation.

He had her own words to use against her. She'd argue him into the ground, but the woman wouldn't dare argue with herself.

Lace grabbed up her cape and whipped it on. Tonight's show had brought her to her senses. She was filled with renewed reason, refreshing anger. How dare Daniel walk away from her—allow *her* to walk away—without letting her tell him how she felt? Didn't he want to know?

The thought that until just moments before, she hadn't even known how she felt flitted in her mind, but she pushed it aside. Her actions were her own, and she was accountable for them, but he had to be accountable for his, as well. She intended to go to him now, tonight. He'd hear how much she loved him if she had to hit him on the head to make him listen. And she'd demand to know if he'd missed her at all, if he wanted to spend more time with her.

All her adult life she'd spoken openly of the pleasure to be found from sexual involvement, but she'd been a fool. Yes, there was pleasure, but it went beyond what she'd thought possible. She loved Daniel, and that made his every touch, even his every look, something special, something that affected her and filled her and became a part of her. She hoped he felt just a little of the same. She suspected he did, and she hoped he wouldn't rally against it just because of who she was and what she did. She couldn't change, wouldn't change, not for him or anyone else. She was proud of herself and her accomplishments, but she wanted him to be proud, too.

If it was at all possible, she intended to find out.

The night was cold and black, the moon hidden behind thick clouds. Lace said good-night to the guard at the front door of the station and headed outside, only to be pulled up short on the front step by a familiar form, a cherished voice.

Daniel stepped out of the darkness and gripped her arms. "I have to talk to you, Lace. Tonight. And don't argue with me."

She threw back her head. The wind tossed her cape and she shivered but ignored the discomfort of the cold. "Why not? I enjoy arguing with you. I'd love to argue with you until I'm too old to manage it anymore."

She waited to see what he would say, what he would do. He stepped closer and the warmth of his body touched her; she could smell his wonderful unique scent, mixed with the smell of the brisk cold and the dampness that hung in the air. It filled her, swirling in her belly and making her ache. She added without thinking, "God, I've missed your scent. And your nearness. And you."

She wrapped her arms around him and pulled him close, pressing her nose into his throat, opening her mouth against his chilled skin, tasting him, suddenly wanting to eat him alive.

Daniel shook. "Lace…" He didn't say anything more. He cupped her face, almost roughly, and pulled her mouth up to his. He kissed her until her body felt weak and she laughed.

"I never thought that was true, never thought it could happen."

He kissed her face, the bridge of her nose, her ear. "What?"

"I thought it was a silly romantic cliché that a woman's knees would go weak. But mine have."

"Mine, too." He kissed her again, his tongue thrusting deep and his hands sliding down to cuddle her bottom, to pull her closer still and support her. "Everything in me feels weak when I'm with you. But strong, too. Like I could take on the world."

"Daniel…"

Suddenly he stepped back and his hands were on her arms again. To her surprise, he shook her, and his voice was enraged. "You're not a hypocrite, Lace. You're intelligent and honest and I insist you stop being so damned stupid!"

"I'm intelligent but stupid?"

"You know what I'm talking about." He shook her again, and because she was so enthralled by his uncharacteristic display, she allowed it. "You told that woman on the radio tonight to be honest. You told her all about love. You have to believe in love or else you're lying not only to yourself, but to your audience, to all those people who rely on you."

Lace stared up at him, bemused, barely able to make out his features in the darkness. "I believe in love."

His hands tightened and he started to shake her again, then he paused. "What did you say?"

"If you weren't so busy trying to rattle my brains, you'd have heard me the first time. I love you, Daniel."

She threw it out there, attached negligently to her

other words, hoping the flow of all the words together would make her declaration less conspicuous. She waited, breathless, for his reaction.

His reaction came swiftly, and was somewhat expected. He kissed her, hard, his mouth moving over hers, devouring. He squeezed her tight against him. "I love you, too. Don't ever do this to me again."

Lace shoved back from him. "I didn't do anything to you! You're the one who played games and pretended and…"

He kissed her again, stopping only to laugh when she lightly punched him in the stomach. "I'm going to kiss you every time you try to pull away from me. You might as well give up. You said you love me and there's no going back. I won't let you go back. You're mine now and I'm going to do with you as I see fit—"

"Ha! From the very beginning, you've always done as you saw fit! That's part of…"

His mouth smothered her words and she ended up laughing too. "I'd cry *uncle,* but I approve of your methods. Will you marry me, Daniel?"

It had worked the first time, tossing out her thoughts in the progression of other thoughts. This time proved just as successful. Daniel picked her up off her feet and swung her around.

She expected a fulsome agreement from him, given his physical display, but to her surprise, and worry, he set her down and bent low to look her in the eye. The brisk wind ruffled his dark hair and chafed his cheeks. His glasses were dotted with melting snowflakes. "There will be problems, Lace."

Her stomach twisted, but she was determined to face the facts, to take her own advice and be brutally honest. "I know it. And I can't promise to change, Daniel. I won't change. My mother did everything she could to suit her husband, and it left her lost. She wasn't herself anymore, but she didn't know who she should be without him.''

His smile was tender and pained. ''You're not your mother, honey, and I don't want you to change. Ever. I love the woman you are. Don't you know that yet?''

Her heartbeat slowed, her pulse became sluggish. ''You don't mind what I do?''

''I listened tonight. And I felt proud. And thrilled, because I knew I had you, I knew you couldn't lie to that woman and tell her all about love unless you believed it yourself. You've just been…skittish because of your mother.''

Lace went on tiptoe. ''Don't start analyzing me again.''

''How about I analyze myself instead, then?''

She waved a hand at him, indicating he should continue.

''I've been scared to death of you, Lace. My father fell apart after my mother died, and it was like living with a shell of a man, no life in him, no laughter or caring for anyone but his own grief. He's still not the same, though he pretends to be. I saw how it had destroyed him, and I didn't ever want it to be that way with me. I could always keep a distance with women, could put on a show of being social, but I held back so much. Then you showed up and you argued with me about everything and stirred me until I was blind with lust, and still, even though I thought I didn't like you, I couldn't put you out of my mind. You obsessed my brain and all my male parts and I hated it.''

''Did you hate me?''

''I was too busy fantasizing over what I'd do with

you to hate you. And then you got hurt and it was like taking a sucker punch in the stomach. I got to know you, and everything changed and I realized I didn't have to worry about falling for you because I didn't think you'd ever fall for me.''

"You were wrong.''

"I know.'' He grinned. "You love me. Max explained it all to me.''

"Oh, to have been a fly on the wall when that conversation took place.''

Daniel laughed, his breath gusting out in front of him in a white cloud. The wind whistled and Lace huddled deeper into her cape. She was cold, but she wouldn't pull her booted feet from the snow until she'd heard it all. This was more than she'd ever hoped for—and she wanted to commit every word to memory.

"Max can tell you all about it later. But for now, will you come home with me?''

"I have my car here.''

"We can get it tomorrow. Tonight I need you.'' His tone dropped, grew husky and seductive. "It's been a lifetime.''

More like two lifetimes, she thought, those words enough to satisfy her. She turned to go back inside. She told the night guard that her car would be left in the lot, so no one would worry, and walked back out to Daniel. They made it to his home in record time. And minutes after that, they were in bed together, their clothes scattered, their bodies straining together.

Daniel moved over her gently, rhythmically, holding himself in check, watching her face. "Tell me again.''

Lace, swamped in pleasurable sensation, struggled to pull her thoughts together enough to form coherent

words. "I love you." Her voice rasped and she threw
her head back, her body arching up high against his.

Daniel kissed her throat. "That's it, Lace. That's it."

She sank her fingertips deep into his shoulders. When
the pleasure finally abated, she forced her eyes open and
stared up at him. "Why didn't you join me?"

"I'm having fun just watching for now." He pulled
her legs higher around his waist and rested. "I can't
believe you love me."

"It defies logic, I know, but it's true."

"Witch." He thrust, a slow, even stroke, and Lace
gasped, giving Daniel reason to smile in satisfaction.
"When can we get married?"

"I'd marry you now, Daniel, if you could manage it.
I love you. Believe me, nothing will change that. You're
the most incredible man I've ever known."

"You don't think I'm too conservative and boring?"

"I think you're too sexy for rational womankind, and
intelligent beyond measure, and so caring and loving and
good—"

"Stop!" His laughter gave her pleasure and she tightened herself all around him. "Next thing I know, you'll
be trying to canonize me."

"No, I want you alive and healthy and hearty," she
said, moving beneath him, watching his expression shift,
his gaze grow hotter, "so you can finish what you've
started."

"You always did present a convincing argument."

A few minutes later Lace grumbled a complaint when
she couldn't find a blanket on the bed. They were all on
the floor and she was getting cold now that they weren't
quite so active. Daniel, mostly dead to the world and
any problems in it, pulled her close and threw one leg
over hers. Lace snuggled up to his side.

Lace thought he was asleep until his low voice filled her ear. "Will you use me as data for the next book?"

She snorted, then smoothed her hand over his hairy chest. "Maybe, but not in the way you hope."

"You plan to ignore my awesome lovemaking techniques? Wasn't that you who swore I was the greatest lover alive, who touted my every move, who—"

"Stop bragging, Daniel. I intend to be the sole beneficiary of your expertise." She levered herself up on an elbow and stared down at him. "But I do think I've learned a great deal about love. I understand now that it comes in various disguises, and that love can't be second-guessed."

He eyed her serious expression. "Because I feared it and you didn't believe it existed?"

"Exactly." It still unnerved her just a bit to discuss it, to realize how close she'd come to losing Daniel out of sheer stubbornness. "We both believed love, in whatever context, was to be avoided. But no matter how hard we both tried, we fell in love anyway."

"I didn't stand a chance. You berated me and wore me down and flaunted your charms until I lay helpless and unable to defend myself." He began toying with her breast, his expression enthralled. "I think of all those wicked things you did to me at the cabin, and I…"

Lace tightened her fingers in his chest hair, challenged him with a look, and waited.

Daniel took the precautionary method of holding her wrist and then kissed her nose. "And I fell in love."

Lace laughed. "A smart man always knows when to quit."

His arms went around her waist. "Ah. But an even smarter man always knows when to begin again." So saying, Daniel flipped her onto her back and grinned down at her. "Now, where were we?"

Lace touched his face, his shoulders. She loved him so much, she knew there couldn't be anything threatening in her feelings, only happiness and contentment. She kissed his grinning mouth and whispered, "We were about to begin the rest of our lives."

"Hmm. Then we should definitely start things off right."

Lace found out exactly what he meant, and she had to applaud his decision. Making love with Daniel, holding him close and hearing his whispers of love was the very best beginning she ever could have imagined.

* * * * *

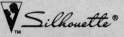

This March Silhouette is proud to present

Silhouette®

SENSATIONAL

MAGGIE SHAYNE
BARBARA BOSWELL
SUSAN MALLERY
MARIE FERRARELLA

This is a special collection of four complete novels for one low price, featuring a novel from each line: Silhouette Intimate Moments, Silhouette Desire, Silhouette Special Edition and Silhouette Romance.

Available at your favorite retail outlet.

Silhouette®